THE
WANDERING STAR

THE VEGA CHRONICLES

A.L. MENGEL

THE VEGA
CHRONICLES

Parchman's Press, LLC, United States of America

COPYRIGHT DISCLAIMER

For mehki –

The One Who Wanders Among the Stars.

THE BOOKSHELF

Ashes Parts I-IV (The Transformation, Dirty Little Secrets, The Coming of the Green Mist, Nesmaron's Egg)

The Quest for Immortality

The Blood Decanter

Curtains and Fan Blades

The Other Side of the Door

#Writestorm

BELOVED FRIENDS,

I had no intentions of writing this novel.

It was a quite unexpected jolt of inspiration that brought on the formation of this story. I had always thought of myself as a Horror Novelist. Paranormal Fiction, mostly. I always had fun with the supernatural, and thought about how I might apply that to science fiction, another passion of mine.

This book challenged my researching and writing abilities like no other has in the past. I chose to step outside my comfort zone, and tell a story that, for me, was something I had not written about before. I had to train my mind to think differently – and to write different words that I had not written before.

The inspiration for this story hit me directly, all at once. It was during the period after *The Blood Decanter* had been submitted to the publisher, and I had chosen to take several weeks off from writing. I needed to decompress after writing such an intense story. At the time, I felt creatively drained. I needed a break.

But then, after a very brief period, I felt the twinge of inspiration for this story. *The Wandering Star* was initially envisioned as a short story. I felt, at the time, that I would begin my Science Fiction storytelling career with a short. Easy to manage. But then, as I sat and wrote, I knew that things were growing.

And so I used my *Writestorm* methodology of writing, and started with a blank, composition notebook page. I pondered about the characters, and they started speaking to me. They told me that this story was far wider in scope than a simple short story. So I then thought that this might be a novella. It wasn't until weeks later, while writing, that I knew this would be a novel.

And then a series.

So enjoy *The Wandering Star*, the little story that grew…and grew.

- A.L.

THE
WANDERING
STAR
THE VEGA CHRONICLES

A.L. MENGEL

PART ONE

THE SHIFT OF
THE SEAS

MANY OF THOSE who remained living on the planet Earth could still remember the days when the oceans shifted towards the poles; and when the sea levels rose, higher, seemingly before their eyes, but certainly within a generation.

For the citizens of the planet, their memory of the water shifting was real and recent; and even years and decades later, many would recall the *Great Shift*. It became dinner table talk, bedtime stories. Those who were too young to remember the period of the *Great Shift* were told of the days when the wave came.

In those days, it was when the mass exodus from the Northern states was plastered over every news channel; every blog; throughout the internet and on every street corner. In the years during which the shift took place, and as the rotation of the planet slowed, the coastal population was forced to relocate to inland cities. Those in the Northern Hemisphere (and equally so in the Southern Hemisphere) would relocate a short distance from their previous coastal residence, and then, several years later, would be forced to move once again, as the sea crept closer...and closer...to the population.

As the planet slowed even further, and it became inevitable for those located nearest to the poles that their cities were slowly being inundated and swallowed by the Earth's waters, it came to a point that entire countries had to be abandoned as great cities were reclaimed by mother nature.

The people of the planet recalled watching in horror as the waters retreated from the tropical zones and spilled towards the north. It wasn't until the northern cities were completely swallowed, and each metropolis would fall into memory and would lie beneath vast depths of seawater, that the inhabitants of the remaining dry areas towards the equator felt the twinge of uncertainty.

Until then, when the cities were lost, it had simply been disbelief.

Some cites, like Atlanta or Rome, with a more southerly location, were not spared entirely from the assault of the waters, but the skyscrapers, and some crests on taller buildings rose from the sea. Those cities were partially inundated and still abandoned. Others, closer to the poles, were completely submerged – under a mile of water in some cases, and sentenced to decompose in a watery grave. London, New York, Toronto, and Moscow – all were lost. Santiago, Sydney, Cape Town…all underwater.

Forever.

The cities closest to the equator were also not spared.

For there, where there had once been oceans, now faded away to new, vast swaths of land as new arid deserts were born on a massive super-continent which reached around the center of the planet, spanning the equator. Once tropical zones, the land was no longer fertile; nor was it habitable. It was a harsh, sandy landscape with a blistering, relentless sun. The failing troposphere caused increasing radiation levels in these areas during sunlight; the levels lowered during darkness.

The super-continent was devoid of water, for the seas which had once surrounded cities like Havana and Mumbai, had flowed towards the poles. Areas that had once had healthy water tables experienced extreme dry conditions; muddy swamps became sandy deserts as the face of the land changed as the ocean retreated.

The phenomenon, which created new inland cities, once coastal communities, blessed with sea breezes, now were landlocked, dry and hot, many miles from the nearest water; and the air, which had thinned tremendously in the center regions of the planet, became unbreathable as the atmospheric layer of gases, which once blanketed the planet, faded. For the sun – once a harbinger of warmth and sustenance – shined at such a ferocity as to cook any mammal or reptile, and serve as a catalyst for radiation from a dying sun heading towards supernova.

Millions perished around the world, either by drowning, asphyxiation or starvation. There were some that heeded the apocalyptic warnings.

Many others maintained a sense of complacency.

The newscasts barked almost constantly about the impending doom, but until the water spilled over the shores of the coasts, and until the radiation had been felt and measured through a decomposing atmosphere, the people of the planet ignored the problem.

Until the problem became insurmountable.

It was not a cinematic horror like on the film medium; people did not tear into the streets and burn up in the sun; their skin did not boil, or slither off of their bones, nor burn and char. But the population was forced to abandon the cities closest to the equator and develop cities beneath the surface of the planet.

But there were some that ignored the warnings; their stubbornness against the reports and subsequent denial served as a catalyst for their demise – and on one particular day, the ocean rose dramatically in a very short period of time. The surge came forth like that of a cataclysmic hurricane; a giant wave was spotted in the ocean, speeding towards the coasts of the world, flowing towards the north and south poles, threatening to flatten any remaining infrastructure; for the rotation of the planet had slowed to a point that it had nearly stopped.

The wave only gave enough warning for the newscasts to break the news – *World's Coastlines Inundated* – and shortly after that, the deed had been done.

Millions drowned who didn't heed the warnings; the warnings of the event were many, and provided over the course of decades, if not longer. Scientists insisted that the slowing of the Earth's rotation could *very well possibly* reach a point where it would slow significantly in a short amount of time, creating massive tsunamis throughout the planet as the oceans displaced.

Man knew that this cataclysmic event was on the horizon, yet it was not understood.

Many could recognize the signs, over the years, indicating that the event was already in progress. But man – as an entirety – did not understand the cause behind the sudden acceleration, whether it was a slow build to a dramatic crescendo, or a sudden, unprecedented cataclysm of change; no matter who commented on the events, whether it be the slow transition or the sudden shift, it did not matter who it was, whether it was those who had been educated their entire lives on the topic, or which stellar University he or she had attended, or how specific a Degree; or how many decades of research they had performed no matter how generalized or specific. It was beyond scientific explanation and reach of man.

No one knew *why* the change in the planet was taking place, nor did they understand the direct cause of the shift of the oceans. Many who populated the planet during the years of the *Great Shift* had been studying it (or at least witnessing it) their entire lives, and the generation before them had already witnessed changes in the coastlines – beaches closer towards the poles were getting smaller, while those near the equator were enlarging. But as one generation passed the torch to the new, the problem remained: Had the Earth been truly slowing its rotation? And what was causing it to happen?

Man did not know, nor did man understand, but the scientists knew the wave was coming. For some phenomenon was slowing, and eventually stopping the rotation of the planet, and the hypotheses had been plentiful and the theories were many.

But when the period of the *Great Shift* arrived, all the people of the planet knew was how to get out of the way, and find new, more hospitable places to live.

The wave wiped out all coastal cities in the Northern Hemisphere, along with cities in the Southern Hemisphere – in particular those closest to Antarctica and others cities inland. Rivers and tributaries, especially those linked to oceans, even indirectly, and well from the main bodies of water, flooded catastrophically.

And while the water initially retreated, it was a sudden surge of water; a gigantic wave, similar to a tide rolling into shore, but on a global scale, forming a new, massive super-continent which spanned the center of the Earth, spanning the equator, reaching thousands of miles from the North Ocean to the South Ocean. After the *Great Shift*, the terrain was like none of the survivors had ever seen before.

There were those who did not perish in the shift. Others died in the south from the exposure to an unforgiving sun nearing death and supernova; cities near the equator baked in temperatures which soared to several hundred degrees Fahrenheit. With the protective layer above the planet in those areas nearly dissipated completely, those who ventured out into the sunlight were burned severely within minutes or exposed to patches of radiation.

Beloved cities located near the equator – Miami, Caracas, Barcelona and Cairo, among many, many others – all were nearly abandoned, surrounded by miles of relentless, barren land, with soaring temperatures that no human could withstand, for a minimum of six months of every year, as the rotation of the planet came to a full and complete stop.

Underground colonies began forming across the center of the new super-continent.

During the period of the initial shift and before the *Great Shift*, vast underground colonies were built and established underneath cities that were becoming increasingly dry as the years passed; elevators had been dug and built, which led to lower levels, each level an expansive colony in and of itself, with artificial light, vegetation, housing and a recycled environment, as the skilled were able to use a vast array of equipment and resources available to construct these underground colonies; those who had been in cities inundated by the wave used their skills to develop the underground cities near the equator. And over the years, the colonies developed, completely underground, as the cities above wasted away. The levels were carved in the ground, the filtered air was recirculated throughout the colony, along with indoor parks. Artificial sunlight was added, and the new below-ground cities were completely self-contained.

As the Earth started to die outside, and as the conditions above ground became increasingly toxic, inside the walls, in cities where the water table had once been too high for a simple basement, people now had their own self-contained culture beneath a skeleton of abandoned skyscrapers and neglected buildings.

But that had been years ago.

And man reached a point where the colonies were no longer sufficient. Supplies were running short, and the colonies struggled to sustain themselves. The environment on the planet above ground was getting increasingly hostile as the rotation of the planet continued to slow, and eventually had been expected to stop altogether. During those years, especially during the years when the supplies were getting dangerously low, rumors of a 'habitable zone' outside – on the Earth, on the surface, in the fresh air, in a green and lush landscape – started to circulate throughout the colony.

Some of the remaining survivors in other colonies were rumored to have traveled to the 'habitable zone', which was thought to be an area of the planet believed to still be able to support human life. That there was an area on the new, super-continent that was still protected by an atmosphere that was still intact; that there were others who were already there, colonizing the land, and that the temperatures were more moderate and tolerable.

Discussions took place – and those who were rumored to have found the area were thought to have traveled through miles of treacherous earthquakes – land splitting in fissures, through ferocious sandstorms and tremendous gaps as hot lava spilled out in locations that had never previously experienced any seismic activity.

But those who did venture out, those who did not initially seek the habitable zone, did so under great duress, and on some days, did not make it far, and were forced to return. The travelers could not leave in the sunlight – for it was too hot. Radiation from the sun seeped into the atmosphere from a weakening atmosphere without warning, and the months of light became deadly. So they could only leave during the six months of darkness, for during the six months of daylight, temperatures soared to several hundred degrees. The months of darkness, however, were unforgiving in their own right. Temperatures plunged well below freezing in the equatorial regions of the Earth; and with a new, unexplored, undiscovered terrain, thousands of miles from Ocean to Ocean, those assumed that those who *did* venture out either succumbed to the freezing temperatures, or became lost in new, uncharted land.

And so during the debate about the existence of the habitable zone, there were those who managed to survive living underneath the southern cities. Their resources were low, and rationed, and more often than not, many went hungry.

And water was scarce.

Fights broke out, almost daily, over something so small as a bottle of water or a loaf of bread. But still, despite the regression, the survivors managed to build a new society of sorts, and started living in an underground catacomb during the months of sunlight – for if they ventured above the earth, they would surely be baked alive.

And during the months of darkness…when the earth froze…could be their only hope for survival…

PART TWO

ARRIVAL OF
THE SCOUT

T HERE WAS A GROUP of survivors gathered around a large, long, wooden dining table, in the center of a stone, windowless room.

Candles burned in the center of the table, and there was a spread of bread and some vegetables in various sized bowls and plates lined in a row along the center of the expansive table. An equal distribution of men and women lined the table, chatting among one another; families with children, babies and the elderly.

All dined together; all were strangers when they first came to the catacombs, now they knew each other, from days, months and years of living next to one another. They rejoiced together in the birth of a newborn; they mourned together in the loss of an elder.

"*It's a myth!*"

One of the elders – who appeared to be the leader of the group – looked up from a plate of potatoes and vegetables and raised his silver eyebrows. He sat back and looked over at the younger, portly man who had shouted the outburst.

The elder tossed his fork on the table with a clank. "You think the habitable zone is a…*myth?*"

The elder scoffed and shook his head as the younger man looked around the room nervously, and sat down slowly. He stood and he tossed his fork on his plate with a clank and looked around the room.

He walked towards the outer wall, looking away from the table. His hands were clasped behind his back, as he looked down at the floor, and stood, for a few moments, and nodded, as the chatter had died down and the room became silent.

He took a deep breath and sighed.

He looked up towards the ceiling, and then turned around and looked back at those dining at the table.

They stopped and looked up at him as he spoke. "The habitable zone is *not* a myth," he said, looking around the room. "I have been in contact with those who have found it. There are people living there already!"

"And how do you know this?" His face shifted. "Have you been there? You have taken the journey?"

The Elder's face froze. "We have received word from some of the other colonies that this area exists. On this new super-continent that we live on. Somewhere, but it hasn't been mapped."

The colonists looked at each other as the room swelled with chatter. The elder raised his arms. "Please…please. All I know are from the communications from those who have contacted me from their zones and, yes, word has traveled."

One of the younger men at the far end of the table stood. He was tall yet muscular, a light blonde, short, military style crew cut. "Elder Cane, a question if I may. How long have you known this, sir?"

Elder Cane nodded. "Good question, Jeremiah. I have announced this revelation at our dinner this evening as I learned from a scout who arrived earlier this morning that a colony in the center of the country has discovered that there is a habitable zone – an area where life can still sustain itself. Outside of the colony. On the surface! Away from the radiation. Where there is still some protection from the sun rays. The temperatures there are warmer than they once were on Earth, but they are tolerable. And life, apparently, is evolving." Jeremiah spoke as he sat back down. "Will it still be the same as here? With the daylight and everything? And the darkness? The cold?"

The others looked on as the elder took a deep breath. "If you mean the length of the sunlight versus night, yes, we expect it to be the same. As many of you know, when this great shift of the seas happened, it happened slowly. Over time, everyone. Of course those of you who are younger will not remember the Old World, those of you who were small children when admitted to the colony and those who were born here in medical. We just noticed it when the air became unbreathable. And the heat was just too unbearable. And when the radiation came, the daylight became deadly."

A large woman, holding a nursing baby, looked up at Elder Cane. She brushed her bushy red hair away from her forehead and looked directly at Cane with wide eyes. "So you are saying we're still going to have six months of daylight there? And six months of night?"

Elder Cane shrugged and returned to the table. "I would imagine so. But then, I don't really know, Elsa. None of us know for certain. We have no reason to believe – since the planet is no longer rotating – that anything will be different in this 'zone'. Other than that it's *habitable*. Plants are growing. Livestock is surviving. We believe…from what we have been told…that there is a degree of protection from the radiation. Some remaining troposphere, perhaps. But I don't have much more to report – yet – until I have had some time to interview this visitor. He came unannounced."

Cane continued: "He's in a coma in medical. He arrived here early this morning – and he may have some answers. When he wakes, and after we have interviewed him, I will call a meeting in the hall."

The colonists returned to their dinner, as a man sitting in the corner strummed his guitar.

Cane shook his head as he returned his attention to his plate, but there was an aura of uncertainty in the room, he could tell.

The conversations had quieted.

He heard the clanks of flatware against china as the colonists continued their meal in silence. Just who was this scout? And why was he visiting their colony when the atmosphere was so hostile? How did he survive the journey?

Cane closed his eyes, and hung his head down toward his plate.

He listened, but the room was silent.

There was an occasional clank of the silverware, and perhaps a cough, or someone clearing their throat, but that was all. The guitarist had even stopped strumming.

And then he remembered the silence in Philadelphia.

Years ago.

Those were different days.

When the city was in pandemonium; when the new coastline had been just a few mere blocks from his high-rise condo.

The quiet that had permeated him through the silent nights, as he would look upwards towards the sky, back in the days of his youth when he was in Philadelphia.

He remembered, so vividly, walking out onto the terrace of his Center City high rise apartment. He had a view across the Delaware River, and on that particular night, when the seas had been shifting, he looked over towards the east, towards New Jersey, and all he saw was darkness.

The waves were coming, and getting closer.

No longer were the familiar lights on the other bank of the river; no longer were Camden and Cherry Hill bustling with activity.

Only…darkness…and silence.

And all he had heard that evening was the dull roar of the surf against an otherwise quiet, still night.

Years had passed since the colonists had populated the underground cities.

For some, they had spent their entire lives living underground in the cities closest to the equator; and Desmond Cane had been no exception.

Before the *Great Shift*, he had been stationed at NORAD. But as the rotation of the planet slowed, oxygen levels thinned in the higher elevations, and he had been relocated to Philadelphia.

But the time in the city of Brotherly Love had been short lived, for the rising sea levels gradually inundated the east coast and, when news of the coming wave broke, the pandemonium ensued.

While standing on his balcony in Philadelphia, Cane had lit a cigarette, and as the pop of the match cracked against the still of the night, and the burning of the cigarette embers crackled, and as he blew a cloud of smoke and looked towards the east, he couldn't get the sounds of the surf crashing on a new, nearby beach out of his mind. He could even hear his breath as he blew out a cloud of smoke.

He knew.

He didn't have to watch the panicked reports on the news.

He didn't have to look out at the streets filled with people; for those in the brownstone walkups were already loading their cars, parked on the sides of the streets, as the water surged its way deeper into the city streets with each passing day.

Cars were stacked with items sometimes three or four feet high, and as Cane looked down, watching the people scurry, he took another drag on his cigarette.

Cane knew.

Without a doubt.

The wave was coming.

He shook his head and turned back towards his living room. The newscast reverberated against the stark walls and hardwood floors, but he was not listening to it. It increasingly sounded like babble. There was no more time to go back to the laboratory, nor was there a reason to.

The panic was already spreading.

And the inevitable was already happening.

With the millions of new residents from across the river spread across the eastern half of the state, there was a different aura to the city. Some lived in tents in parks; others, who could afford it, rented apartments or houses in the suburbs.

But none of that mattered anyway.

For the streets that had once bordered the Delaware were swiftly becoming inundated by surging seawater; and soon, millions would be displaced once again…

…Back at the colony dinner, Cane looked up from his plate and scanned the room. "Finish your dinners as you usually do. There is no reason for silence. No need whatsoever. Go ahead, talk amongst your friends. This scout will tell us his intentions when he wakes. Until then, I will not hold anyone accountable for speculation." He looked over at the guitarist and nodded.

The conversations swelled, drowning out the strumming guitar music, as the colonists continued with their dinner.

Jeremiah Walter was also regarded as a leader. And although he sat at a different table from the Elders, his youth did not deter from his knowledge or stature in the colony.

He looked on as the Elders took their seats.

He watched Cane, who had appeared deep in thought. The man was staring down at his plate, sometimes with his eyes closed.

Jeremiah knew what Cane had been thinking about, because he thought about the same things.

He sat back on the hard, wooden bench, and looked around the room. Many of the colonists at dinner had come here either as children, or were born here.

It had been years now since they had all arrived. Some had been here longer than others. But the most recent group of arrivals had been in residency for close to five years.

The authorities said it would only be for a short while.

Until "they could figure out what was going on and what had caused the *Great Shift*".

They had said that the catacombs were a temporary holding facility, until the habitable zone could be located and a mission could be arranged. And it became, over time, that who "they" were had been increasingly unclear.

But that was years ago, and the only thing that had changed was been a planet that had gotten increasingly hostile. And supplies which were getting far more scarce with each passing month and year.

As Jeremiah looked around the room, he saw the Elders, chatting amongst each other, drinking their water and their wine, and then he looked over towards the commoners, who were seated on benches across a long, slender table. Had they been sentenced to this indefinitely? And how many of them had known only this existence?

He closed his eyes for a moment, and listened to the chatter about the room. The clanking of flatware against plates, the indiscernible chatter of conversations that if were not honed in on, swiftly became the clatter of noise.

In his mind, he heard the conversations from the crowds outside the doors. The chatter in the dining room forced him to remember. He could feel the searing sun blistering his neck and back. There hadn't been much time left. And when he looked up, he drew his arm up to cover his eyes.

"Name!"

He looked up.

A security officer dressed in green stared at him, his forehead shifted. He held a brown clipboard with paperwork. He held his hands out after a few minutes of silence. "Do you hear me?" he said. "Are you coming to the catacombs, or not?"

Jeremiah looked down, shook his head, and laughed nervously. "Uh…yes. My family should be inside? Right?"

The guard looked down at his clipboard. "You said your last name was Walter?"

Jeremiah nodded and shifted his backpack from his right arm to his left.

"I don't see that name on here."

Jeremiah's shoulders dropped and his bag fell to the ground. He stepped forward as the guard looked up at him and raised his eyebrows, but did not move. "Step back."

Jeremiah took a step back and shook his head. He pointed towards the clipboard. "Check it again, please. We are on the list."

The guard shook his head and sighed, but did not look back up at Jeremiah for several minutes. Finally, he pursed his lips and raised his eyes to look at Jeremiah. "I don't see them sir."

Jeremiah took a few steps back, and looked up towards the sky.

He held his arms out, and looked the common area: there were lines of people, families for the most part, which led up to the row of tables in front of the building – a large, imposing cement and steel structure, with multiple doors that appeared to be cargo bays, but each of the doors were closed. In front of each door was a table, and group of doctors dressed in white coats.

He stormed a table, slamming his palms down on the wood. "Look around! All families here!

Do you not see them? Have you seen them?"
A surprised doctor looked at him with wide
eyes and lay his clipboard down on the table.
"Sir what is your name? Are you on the list?"
"Jeremiah Walter."

Jeremiah took a step back and clasped his
hands down in front of his legs as he saw a
group of guards, dressed in blue, approach the
table. The tallest was an older man with silver,
stringy receding hair. "What seems to be the
problem here, James?"

The doctor looked over at the group of guards.
"I don't think he is on the list, Elder. Walter.
That's his surname. I am not seeing him. I
cannot examine him if he isn't on the list."

Jeremiah looked at the man directly. The man's
stringy hair looked familiar.

Like he had seen the man before, in a different
time and place, most likely a completely
different context – he may have stood behind
the man at the Shop 'n' Save, or perhaps they
gassed their cars next to one another.

But Jeremiah had the distinct feeling that he
had laid his eyes on the man, at some distant
point in the past.

The silver-haired man looked over at Jeremiah, who stood and looked directly back at him.

"You're not on the list?"

Jeremiah shook his head and ran his hands over his bald head. "No, sir. I received the certification in the mail last week. I have it in my pocket."

Jeremiah dug through his pocket and produced a dirty, wrinkled paper, and held it out in front of the guards. The eldest looked down as another guard next to him reached for it, and slowly unfolded it. The eldest man retrieved a pair of glasses from his front pocket and looked down at the document, studying it for several minutes, until he removed his glasses, folded them, and placed them back in his pocket. "I see that there are supposed to be three others besides you."

Jeremiah nodded.

"So where are they?"

He shrugged and looked around.

The eldest shook his head. "The requirements are given quite clearly, Mr. Walter. Since you were expecting the invitation, you should have seen on the newscasts that the entire list of invitees must be present for anyone to be admitted."

"So what are you saying then? I can't locate them so I have to go back out there and burn in the sun?"

The old man raised his eyebrows and looked at Jeremiah. "Now you know that those months will not be here for at least another six weeks. Until then, there is a period when you can safely move about in the light. It's like morning right now. The sun isn't as strong as it is in mid-day. You can certainly find another colony before then."

Jeremiah stopped for a moment and looked at the eldest man, who took the wrinkled document, folded it in thirds and handed it back to him.

"I know you from somewhere," Jeremiah said. "I know I have seen you before."

The eldest man raised his eyebrows and looked at Jeremiah directly.

"Name's Cane. I am the Director of this installation. Desmond Cane. I've been involved with NORAD out in Colorado and more recently, was stationed in Philadelphia when the waterline shifted. And, of course, I oversaw the creation of this colony."

Jeremiah's eyes widened. "*That's* where I knew you from!" He took a step forward and extended his hand as Cane took a cautious step back. Jeremiah followed by taking a few more steps forward. "I saw you on the news up there! Quite a few times, actually!"

"How, may I ask?"

"I lived in New Jersey. Grew up there, at least before we were displaced by the wave."

Cane nodded and looked at his clipboard. "And where did you go when New Jersey was overcome with the surge?"

"I went with my family to Philadelphia for some time. But then we scattered."

Cane nodded. "How old are you?"

"Older than you think. And older than I look."

Cane looked up from his clipboard and looked Jeremiah up and down, and then settled his eyes directly looking in Jeremiah's. "Even so, even if you are decades older than you look, you would have been a child when the *Great Shift* happened. You may know New Jersey, but it hasn't existed for a very long time."

Jeremiah placed his hands on his hips and studied the man. "I remember you, Mr. Cane. I saw you on the news. I may have been a child, but I remember that. Just like I remember getting a bright, shiny red firetruck for my third birthday. And I remember throwing up in class the following year. There are memories that just stick with you."

Cane nodded slowly, never taking his eyes off the new arrival. He looked on at the young, energetic man. "Very well then."

Jeremiah had wondered why there was so much distrust.

He remembered Cane quite vividly now; and although Philadelphia had then been inundated – at least to the point of waves lapping at the third and fourth floors of downtown skyscrapers, he remembered Cane leading a great percentage of the population of Philadelphia to safer, dry land.

But that had been before man fully understood what had been happening in the world. And until the colonies were built underneath the southern cities, there were groups of the population who became nomadic; others had become marooned in buildings surrounded by a new, swirling ocean.

"Why weren't they rescued?"

Cane paused for a moment.

He cocked his head to the side and shifted his face, leaning his head closer towards where Jeremiah was standing. "Come again?" He raised his eyebrows.

Jeremiah looked directly back at Cane. "Those who were trapped in the buildings. Why were they not rescued?"

"You were just a child when this happened! How dare you question *me*!"

Jeremiah folded his arms. "I may have been a child then, but I am far from a child now. And my memory is long, Mr. Cane. I remember the days after we went to Philadelphia. And then after that when we fled south."

Cane straightened, took a deep breath, and sighed. He looked directly at Jeremiah.

"The shift was unprecedented. And when the big shift happened – when the water came like a tsunami – that is when it became too dangerous. There were those that heeded our warnings. And the others…those in denial…unfortunately there was nothing we could do for them at that point."

Jeremiah scoffed. "You've answered this question before, haven't you?"

Cane had seemed like he had given a planned, rehearsed response.

Cane nodded. "Of course. Millions perished. But it was not because of *me*. It was because of the cataclysmic event. When the oceans washed away the poles, there were millions stranded in marooned skyscrapers – short on supplies and with no way for the survivors to reach them. The Earth is a force that we still do not fully understand. And when we learned about the inevitable, we tried to convince them to leave. They didn't want to. And they died because of it."

"Why wouldn't they want to leave when they saw the ocean filling the streets before their eyes?"

Cane handed his clipboard to one of his assistants and took a step closer to Jeremiah. He held his finger out, pointing it directly at the young man's face. "You listen here to me, boy. If you want in this colony, you better stop questioning me. I have given you answers, which I had no reason to give you in the first place. I am the Director of this colony! I don't answer to you! If you want in, you'd better start showing some *damned* respect!"

Jeremiah looked at Cane but each said nothing. The noise around them – scattered voices, feet crunching through gravel – continued, but seemed distant as the two men watched each other, waiting for one to speak.

Cane folded his arms across his chest. "If you want to stay at this colony, sir, you have to submit to a thorough examination. Medical but also metaphysical. We have an observation process – which touches on both the real and the abstract. We use it to determine the motives of all new arrivals who come alone. Especially with the nature of your questions."

Jeremiah nodded as Cane extended his hand. "Then if you agree to the procedure, let me welcome you to the colony. On a probationary basis, of course, pending the results of your evaluation."

Jeremiah nodded as he shook the leader's hand. "Of course." Their grip was firm and tight.

Jeremiah waited as Elder Cane and the two guards retreated. The doctor looked up from the table. "Wait here, sir. There will be some medical personnel who will come by to take you to the examination room."

A team of doctors and nurses led Jeremiah through the expansive hydraulic doors, and deep into the hallways and into a clearly labeled medical area, as one of the many assistants, a small dark-haired Latino man, tugged Cane's arm as he looked on. "Why did you let him stay?"

"I read his files, Eli. He has an extensive background which we can use. You know why we are recruiting in the first place, right?"

Eli nodded.

"Good then," Cane said, patting Eli on the back. "Now maybe you will understand why, sometimes, we have to let people in who we don't exactly agree with on every single topic. And of course he will be medically and metaphysically vetted just like any other new recruit."

Eli nodded again as the two men walked into the catacomb. "I understand sir. But he's a pistol. He looks like he could be hard to handle."

Cane stopped walking and looked directly at Eli, who also paused and looked up at Cane. Cane placed his arm on Eli's shoulder and looked him directly in the eye. "Then I sure better hope I can handle him." Cane chuckled, patted Eli on the shoulder, and walked off, leaving his assistant standing dumbfounded and shaking his head.

Several years after Jeremiah had been admitted to medical, when he had been sitting at the dinner with Cane and the other colonists, Cane had announced that there had been a visitor (an unexpected scout whose visit was unprecedented). And on that very same evening, Jeremiah had opened his eyes and looked around the dining room.

The guitarist was still playing as the colonists were finishing their meals, and gradually others rose from their seats and brought their plates to the side clearing area.

He had been at this colony longer than he had planned, but he felt, at least to a degree, that he fit in with the others.

He had come a long way since the day when he stood in the lines, but now, so much time had passed, months, in fact, and the sun would finally be setting soon.

Nearly a half-year of daylight, a sun which could not be enjoyed, wore on everyone. Not too much more time, and there would be the opportunity to venture out – to search for the zone – and their window would soon close again.

For months after the sun set, the sun would again rise, and then, with the brilliance of the unfiltered rays, going outside the colony doors would almost certainly result in severe burns to the skin, and even then, should the skin survive and remain intact, the fight for air, for breathable, clean air, would be hard won.

He knew that with each passing day, the odds became increasingly difficult, for each year, the temperatures increased, and, despite the frigid chill of the dark months, it was during those night time months that their greatest opportunity for a quest would arise, and the time was approaching swiftly.

Jeremiah rose from his seat and walked over to a set of double steel doors on the side of the dining room. He looked over at Cane, who was eating and chatting amongst the other Elders; he was completely unaware that Jeremiah was leaving.

And he slipped quietly out the door.

He peered down the South Corridor towards Medical.

The hallway was empty; but the overhead florescent lights were stark, bright and reflected against the shiny cement flooring. He paused for a moment, leaned against the wall, and listened.

He could hear laughing.

Someone was laughing inside the dining room. A big, billowing laugh, from deep inside the belly.

Jeremiah held his breath and listened again. It was mainly nonsensical chatter, but he heard the laugh again.

Cane.

Jeremiah closed his eyes and shook his head, hanging his neck downwards. The laughter inside the dining room faded away as he remembered. He closed his eyes.

He saw the brilliance of green grass and a flourishing landscape; in his escape into his mind, he was no longer in the colony. He could still smell the fresh air; and the sea salt of the Jersey Shore. No longer were there the cold, hard cement walls, and the elevators that led down, deeper into the underground civilization. No longer did he have to live in artificial light.

The sun had been warm against his skin. Inviting. The call of seagulls coasted through the air.

For when he looked around, he saw the brilliant green grass. The colorful flowers. And when he turned his head towards the sky, the blue was different.

It felt real.

More natural.

Not like the artificial sky on the lower levels of the catacombs.

This was authentic.

And the sun was shining and bright. It felt reassuring.

The sun was real; the sun was friendly.

He looked down at his hands. The scar was still there, from when he was a boy, when he had slit his hand with a kitchen knife. He flipped his hand over and examined the dirt underneath his fingernails. Yes, the reality seemed so authentic.

He looked up towards the sun and shielded his eyes. The sun was shining as it did when he was a boy; when it was warm but not too hot; not piercing.

Jeremiah opened his eyes, and looked down the corridor. He'd had the vision again. He shook it off and looked at the set of steel doors at the end of the hallway.

The scout was down there.

Lying in bed in ME 1.

Jeremiah turned around and cracked the door open to the dining room. The noise from the colonists, intermingled with the guitar music, flowed outwards, but he kept the door open just a fraction. He could feel the cool air flow through the crack against his face. No one noticed him peeking through the sliver. And Cane was engrossed in a conversation and sipping on a glass of red wine.

And then Jeremiah closed the door silently.

He headed down the corridor towards Medical, backing away silently from the dining room doors, and as he got further away, he turned around and picked up speed.

He had to see the scout.

This unexpected visitor.

The one who came without warning.

For he remembered. He thought about his medical examination, from years before.

The star.

Was it the star?

Had the star been guiding him all along? Or was there a connection between the scout and the star?

He could remember it now.

And there was something – a connection – between the star and the scout. There had to be. And then the voice came.

Are you listening to me?

Jeremiah paused when he got to the massive steel doors that led into medical. "Am I what?"

Listening to me.

Jeremiah paused, with his palm on the door, ready to swing it inwards. But it was a familiar voice. It triggered thoughts of his medical exam, back when he had first arrived at the colony. Could it be the same voice?

"Who is that?" He looked up, but it was just the ceiling. Nothing unordinary. There was no opening to the heavens and outer space.

I'm the one who you should be listening to.

Back at one of the earlier colony dinners, Elder Cane had stood in front of the dining table and looked over at Jeremiah, who threw his head back in laughter for a moment, surrounded by younger, female colonists, each hanging on him, looking up at him longingly with puppy dog eyes.

Cane returned his attention to the dinner table, and glanced at some of the other colonists.

Counselor Abagail was at the opposite end of the table chatting with several others from Protection, and, at that point it didn't matter how the young man Jeremiah had wormed his way into the colony.

Cane shook his head, but said nothing, and watched as Jeremiah laughed with his perfect, white teeth, and smiled with the women who attached themselves to his arms.

He was a stupid, silly, young and inexperienced young man. He led with his muscles and his beauty.

The women in the colony flocked to him, as they did that same evening at dinner, and at dinner every evening.

Cane watched Jeremiah as he laughed as the three women looked over at him, expectantly, laughing at every word he said, hanging on his shoulders, looking up into his eyes, and watching his gleaming white teeth as he smiled. They laughed, along with him, and each took a sip of water as Jeremiah had taken a sip of his own water.

Cane returned to his seat, placed his hands on his knife and fork, paused for a moment, and then looked back over at Jeremiah.

And then, at that moment, there seemed to be a connection between the men. When Jeremiah looked up at Cane, they made eye contact, and Cane looked down, sat back down, and stared at his plate.

It didn't used to be like this.

There didn't used to be a young, muscular buck taking over his colony. He used to have full power. Back in his days at NORAD, he *was* that young muscular buck. And he remembered, when Jeremiah first set foot in the colony, after they had confronted each other in the yard, when Jeremiah had stated that he could well handle any physical labor.

And Cane knew the man had a high level of fitness and would be able to withstand the temperature extremes for expeditions.

So Elder Cane had permitted him to stay. "Come with me," Elder Cane had said to Jeremiah, just after he had cleared the admissions table on the day of Jeremiah's arrival.

And when he again watched Jeremiah, he saw the young man stop playing with the women, and the two men could tell they were thinking about the same thing.

Jeremiah followed the senior man, over towards the entry chamber, as the large hydraulic doors opened up towards the ceiling.

The two men walked into a vast, barren hallway. The cement was polished, yet drab and uninteresting. The hallway was wide, stark, and lengthy.

Jeremiah's sneakers squeaked on the polished concrete. Elder Cane walked fast, much faster than one would think an older person would walk, and Jeremiah had to half-walk, half-run to keep up with the man.

Elder Cane turned around to speak to Jeremiah as he walked.

"I allowed you to stay because you claim that you have a penchant for geology, meteorology and astronomy. We need that type of mind in our colony. That scientific way of thinking. And you claim a high level of fitness as well. If this is all to be true, you will be permitted to stay. If not, you will have to leave."

Elder Cane led the way as Jeremiah kept up. "Where are we going?"

Elder Cane did not turn around. "We are heading to a medical facility – state of the art. We have a procedure where you will be sedated and wrapped in a metal skin, which will read all of the impulses of every nerve ending in your body. All of that information will be sent to us and we can look into your mind." Elder Cane paused for a moment as they stood at the corner of several hallways. "And there will be no way to hide," he said. "The mind becomes completely visible under a nerve wrap, and we will discover the truth. You say you want to stay, this is what happens. We do this procedure all the time. It's the latest thing. Total neurological submission, Jeremiah. That's your requirement to join us."

Jeremiah looked straight ahead for a moment, and nodded slowly. "What type of information are you looking for?"

"There are a lot of wanderers out there," Cane said, as he started down a larger, wider hallway. "Now we are living in barren land. Supplies are in abundance in abandoned cities, but with such a short window to retrieve them, colonies are growing desperate. Since the shift, satellites became useless, even maps are obsolete. All we know – and a lot of this theory is largely an assumption – is that we *think* there is a large swath of land spanning the equator, and two new Oceans. One at each pole. But with the planet now uncharted territory, scouts are getting lost. Still, there are those that jump from colony to colony. Try to take over. Steal supplies. And leave." He looked over at Jeremiah with an icy stare. "That's not you. Is it?" Jeremiah quickly shook his head. "No. That's not me. I'm just looking for a colony to join."

"Then you must have your medical and metaphysical exam, as we discussed." They reached the double doors. It was lined with the same, plain stainless steel doors as the others. "By consenting to this procedure, we will determine that you are not a wanderer. A leach. And then, you will have completed the vetting procedure, and you will be able to join the colony."

"And what type of things could indicate failure of the test?"

Cane shrugged and looked over at Jeremiah. "Your mind will tell us, Mr. Walter. But we have to see that your intentions are noble. And that you aren't here to steal supplies and leave off the next day." Cane stopped for a moment, and Jeremiah stood and looked over at the man. Cane placed his hand on Jeremiah's shoulder and looked into his eyes. "About a year or so back, we had a scout come. He wandered in from the city. We had already closed the doors – it was just before the sunrise was to come. He was allowed into the colony without the test."

Jeremiah's eyes widened. "What happened?"

Cane sighed, looked down for a moment, and then back up at Jeremiah. "He had to be exterminated. Recycled. Turns out he was from up towards Atlanta – not sure which colony. But they sent him down here to recruit and steal supplies. Needless to say, we ate well that night."

Jeremiah shook his head.

The two men turned down an even longer hallway.

The floor was the same polished concrete, and the walls were a stark cinder block, with a stainless steel door every few feet.

"This facility was built when the government announced that the rotation of the earth was slowing.

Billions of dollars were poured into this facility, and other facilities across the southern United States.

There wasn't much on these projects in the news. I was elected to run this facility. But that was before everything stopped. And before we lost the north."

"So…these facilities…they compete with one another?"

Cane shrugged his shoulders again. "For supplies? Some do, some don't. Since the great shift, there is no government anymore. Each of the colonies exists on their own. It just kind of faded into that. But now…it's become a quest for survival, and usually just before the sunrise, we get a great migration. Like we did with you. People try to find a better colony when they can move in the darkness, but once that sun rises – forget it. It all stops."

"Why do people seek out new colonies?"

"More supplies, a different way of thinking. It's similar to migrating from one country to another, like people did back in the olden days. Now, people come, some stay. Some move on. We don't force people to stay here. But, occasionally, we get someone who arrives at our doorstep at the brink of death."

Cane stopped and looked over at Jeremiah, directly in his eyes.

Cane smiled. "I think experiencing that convinces them to stay."

They reached a set of double doors at the end of the hallway, and Cane pressed his thumb against a plate on the wall. "We are here for your medical exam."

The two men walked into a medical lab with a large, raised bed in the center, and a stainless steel table, with a large, rectangular center and two smaller steel peninsulas on either side, similar to the shape of a man. Monitors and equipment surrounded the table, along with a set of bright lights, which shined directly down on the examination area. And the rest of the lab was relatively void of furniture or light.

"Undress," Cane said, as they stood next to the table.

Jeremiah looked up at Cane, raised his eyebrows and looked at the man directly. He peeled off his t-shirt, revealing an astonishing level of fitness; he was muscular, but not a beastly monster. The chest muscle was, however, significant and pronounced; he was clearly athletic; his pectorals surrounded a nest of hair in the center of his chest, which reached down towards a rippling mid-section and powerful, roping and vascular legs. His arms flexed as he moved, and as he stripped his jeans, he stood back up and looked over at Cane.

"I told you I was in shape."

"You are quite fit, I see. That will work to your benefit here, should you be selected to stay. Now the rest, please. We must hook you up. And no clothes. None whatsoever."

Jeremiah stood in a pair of brilliant white underwear and looked at Cane, who stood, arms crossed, looking on. "Today please."

Cane raised his hand and ushered several of the medical staff over. They stood on either side of Jeremiah in yellow scrubs, masks and gowns. They reached out and held Jeremiah's arms, and stretched outwards, and guided him back to a chair.

"We will explore your mind," Cane said as the staff assisted him to a table directly under the lights. "And while that is happening, we will also be closely be examining your body. You will not remember much from this event. But

I will share the outcome with you when the procedure has been completed."

Jeremiah was spread out on the exam table, his arms wide, and the medical staff inserted several needles into his arms, and finally, a large cover was wrapped over his body – a bright and reflective foil. The medical staff carefully wrapped it around each limb, wrapping it tightly so it was like a second skin. And then over his torso and chest, and finally around his head. His face was left exposed, and he looked up at Cane expectantly. Cane could see that Jeremiah's eyebrows were shifted with worry. "This is standard procedure," Cane said. "There is no cause for alarm. No cause for concern."

When Cane stepped back from the examination table, a nurse placed an opaque, heavy mask over Jeremiah's face. In the center was a small, round steel plate with a tiny hole in the center.

"Do not worry," Cane said, as he heard rapid breathing underneath the mask. "We will monitor all of your vitals, and you, sir, just need to relax and remember. *Relax.*" He nodded over at the waiting nurse, as one last needle was inserted into the center of the mask, in the waiting receptacle. Several wires were attached at all pressure points on the body – near the wrists, ankles, and remaining joints.

"Do not worry," Cane said, as he exited the room. He could still hear Jeremiah's breathing. "Just remember for me. That is all you need to do right now."

There was a certain darkness after that. Jeremiah was quite lucid; he recalled being in the examination room, lying on the table, and he even remembered the sting of the needles in his arms.

And the striking smell of the alcohol swabs.

And next, when he opened his eyes, he could see only darkness, but he knew exactly how he got there. And then he waited. He was not aware of the passage of time, and when he looked behind him, he did not see anything like people who have experienced a 'Near Death Experience' (NDE's) have claimed: he did not appear to be floating above his body. He did not see a tunnel, he did not appear floating towards any light, which some described would spill into a long, cylindrical tube.

He was just locked in total, complete darkness.

Until there was a miniscule point of light.

In the distance, he could see it.

Like a tiny, white pinprick of light. He had remembered studying in school in the days of his youth – and he remembered someone once telling him that a human eye could see the flame from a burning candle up to thirty miles away. "On a clear night, of course." That had been the stipulation he had remembered hearing. The disclaimer. But the voice reverberated in his head.

And this pinpoint, this tiny white light, seemed so far, yet he was drawn to looking at it. It may have been a star, and it appeared to be moving towards him. As if levitating.

"Is anyone there?"

His voice echoed against the silence.

But the pinpoint of light continued towards him, moving – ever so slowly – but still moving. Jeremiah waited; floated; and attempted to journey towards the light, but could not. He struggled, attempted to swim through the empty space, and was able to make absolutely zero progress.

"Where the heck am I?"

But there was still no answer.

He looked ahead, and saw that the tiny pinprick of light had gotten slightly larger; now, he assumed, it was about the size of a pea. Maybe a pencil eraser. But he could tell it was somehow still moving towards him; the trajectory appeared unchanged. Levitating; hovering in some fashion. When he squinted his eyes, he could see, just a bit more clearly. Some pulsating to the orb, but a clear and definite movement.

Jeremiah knew that the orb – the cosmic being – or whatever it was, looked to be taking its time. And he wondered about the purpose of putting him here, in whatever this darkness was, whether it was some sort of a holding chamber, perhaps for quarantine, he couldn't be clear. And then something permeated his thoughts.

He couldn't help but think about Philadelphia.

All his thoughts were scattered, like tiny puzzle pieces begging to be assembled, floating in front of him; like small fragments of thought, tiny televisions in all shapes and sizes, with color, movement and purpose. But he didn't know where to start.

"Start with the edge pieces first?"

He looked to the left and the right. No change. But as the orb of light grew to the size of the baseball, he saw a wisp of light to his left, and snapped his head in the direction of the traveling globe of white, hot light.

It flashed towards him, and his body flew backwards, sending him into a spin.

And then he remembered the bridge.

The giant, soaring suspension cables reached upwards from the bridge above the Delaware – the one named after that famous poet.

The Walt Whitman.

Jeremiah's eyes remained closed and there was the night that he had remembered on the bridge.

He remembered standing on that very bridge, looking at the stalled traffic in the bright, hot afternoon. The temperature was well above 100 degrees, and he mopped the sweat off his brow. The evacuation traffic from New Jersey was at a critical level; but it wasn't the cars that he saw.

It was the woods. The tops of the trees as fading sunlight filtered through, to the bed of dried, brown leaves below.

"Are you coming?"

That voice he could remember.

A male voice.

Speaking to him. Off to the right. But he couldn't turn his head to see who it was.

It didn't matter.

He didn't have to look towards the voice to see the rush of water flowing through the trees. And then the voice was gone. Swallowed into a new and mighty sea.

His mind loosened, and he saw the suspension cables, as if he were standing on the edge of the bridge. And then he saw the dark, murky water of the Delaware River below; and the buildings rising from the Philadelphia skyline towards the west, like giant, shadowy boxes reaching to the sky, with pinpoints of scattered lights on the sides. There was too much to remember for his mind at that point.

"I need more…" he said. He could feel the pillow underneath the back of his head, and he felt a pinprick on his arm. In a state of semiconsciousness, like the field between sleep and waking, that small, snippets of time in which sounds can be heard, but the body is powerless to do anything – that felt, to him, like where he was. But his mind never left the *Walt Whitman* over the Delaware River; he was nearly there.

It just took that one extra shot.

And then he was there.

His arms and legs splayed outwards as he floated in the darkness. When he had a sense of his body, he saw it was clearly naked, but covered.

He was covered in a skin, like a second skin, a grey epidermis, like a suit, which felt like nothingness. And then, as the light became closer, now about the size a small, round swimming pool, he focused on the sphere.

Jeremiah.

Light and fire fingered out towards the darkness as the star pulsated.

He paused for a moment and considered the swirling beacon of light.

It was pulsating, and not entirely white. He could see faint wisps of color dashing through the diameter of swirling heat, and as he looked towards the outer edge, there was decreased definition.

Jeremiah, are you listening?

There was a certain presence to the light; not overbearing or overpowering in the slightest. But as it grew larger, from the size of a swimming pool to giant proportions; it became engulfing and brilliant.

"Are you…speaking to me?"

Flashes through the light wisped back and forth – some were colorful, others were darker blotches, and even more were brilliant and brighter than the orb itself.

Cosmic dust, as brilliantly white and pastel like the star, swirled around the circumference of the stellar being; and it fingered its way towards him…closer…and closer.

You must listen to me.

He looked over at the sphere of light.

His mouth dropped open, as it hovered closer to his levitating body, and as he looked upwards at the vast size, he could only look, and take in its brilliance and beauty.

You must lead them, Jeremiah.

You have been called here to be their leader. To guide them from their torment.

To be their warrior.

He looked down at his body as he tugged at the neck of the silver skin suit, and shook his head, and closed his eyes.

"I am not a leader."

But you are a leader.

I have called you here, Jeremiah.

I have cleared the path and opened the doors for you to enter. Now, it is up to you to walk through.

Will you answer my call?

He closed his eyes.

Was this the star?

The bright orb of light that he had had been told about as a child? Was this the star that he had watched through his telescope in the days of science class? He remembered the star in those days. That shiny beacon in the night sky, as he craned his neck upwards, he could see it hovering.

It had been brighter than the other stars in the sky.

He had remembered the star quite clearly, and now, before it once again, he took pause.

He opened his eyes and looked at the pulsating globe.

Jeremiah, I have come for you. Only you. Will you answer my call?

"Are you calling me?" His words sounded distant. As if he were levitating in the vastness of space alone; as if the words would not travel nor be heard.

You are called…but not by me.

His eyes remained intense, and the star had flashes of bright, hot white, pale blue, red and orange bursting from it, but it hovered in front of him; it stopped levitating towards him, as if waiting for an answer.

"You have come to deliver me a message?"

The star did not answer.

The hot, white sphere continued hovering close towards him, pulsating with pastel hues in the center.

"You are appearing to me…am I dead? Did I not survive the procedure?"

Jeremiah looked down at his body as he floated in the blackness. And when he looked up, he was surrounded by stars, in the vastness of outer space. The star continued levitating, but then slowly started to retreat, and as Jeremiah's eyes began to adjust to the darkness, he scanned the area: millions upon billions of tiny, white stars, some larger than others.

The star continued its backwards motion.

Turn around and look behind you...

Jeremiah froze, and his eyes widened.

As the star continued to retreat backwards, Jeremiah slowly turned around, and then he knew where he was. It was the area in the galaxy which he had heard about; but it was what was behind him, which he saw when had turned around fully, in that smooth, poetic motion of floating through the galaxy: for he recognized the fields of blue instantly.

The familiarity was washing over him, until he looked closer. Oceans. Continents. Just like the maps he had once remembered.

That was many, many years ago.

Before the rotation stopped.

Do you see what I am trying to show you? Do you understand the purpose?

Jeremiah looked back towards the white star, which had retreated to a point, and then had paused, pulsating and spinning.

"Why are you showing me this?"

The star did not answer, so Jeremiah slowly turned back to face the planet he had thought he knew.

And then he saw, the slow transformation, take place before his eyes. He felt as if he were traveling towards the blue planet, as it grew larger; as if either he were traveling or the planet was moving towards him. The stars around him flashed past, flashing lines of light as his speed increased, until he found himself right in front of Earth, hovering in its orbit.

He floated in the orbit, and as he looked off to his right, he recognized the pale reflection of the moon, and then turned around.

The star was hovering behind him.

Look before you, and watch as I show you.

Jeremiah looked at the planet. He had remembered studying maps when he was a child in geography classes. He could recognize the Atlantic Ocean below where he floated; he had estimated that he was between South America and the Caribbean.

The blue of the oceans started swirling and, at first, just so slightly, he saw a beige line, the terraforming land form across the center of the Earth, near the approximate location of the equator as the water started to move. He snapped his head around and looked at the white pulsating star. "Is this the beginning?"

Watch and you will see, Jeremiah.

He turned around, and the line expanded outwards, as the blue retreated towards the poles, and after a few moments, there was a complete shift of land and water.

"Is this what Earth looks like now?! A giant land mass in the center and massive oceans at the poles?! How did things change like that so quickly?"

He snapped his head around and looked at the star.

It was hovering behind him, pulsating with electron energy, pulsating rays and colors, and then, after silence, the star started to retreat backwards. But he looked over towards the sun.

There was a redness to it that he hadn't quite noticed before. A crimson hue.

Do you seek the answers of what has happened to your planet? And of what is going to happen?

Do you wish to discover what surrounds the confusion that plagues the colonies that now inhabit the Earth?

He stopped and looked at the star.

It continued to pulsate, as if waiting for a response from him.

"The sun. It is dying? Are we sentenced to be the last race? The final intelligent life in the solar system?" He shook his head and turned to look over at Earth. He closed his eyes and lowered his head.

"This is just a dream I am having. Just a bunch of random thoughts. I am not really levitating above the Earth in space. Am I?"

He sighed and opened his eyes once again.

He turned over towards the star. "We certainly would have seen something like this by now. A dying sun?"

Now is the time to journey beyond. To find a new home. For the planet you call home, now, is broken.

Jeremiah felt like he was being pulled, captured in the gravitational pull, and as he turned around he saw the Earth getting smaller, and smaller, as the star pulled him; he felt like he was floating, but in the moment that he closed his eyes, and opened them again, he looked to his right, and saw the fiery red planet Mars. Their speed slowed as Jeremiah looked at the planet that humankind had been striving to reach and colonize before the shift of the seas.

"Is this our destiny? Is it in our fate? To colonize a new planet? Create a new home?"

Jeremiah looked over at the star as a plume of gases shot out of the side.

That is not the answer.

That is the planet that man has been fascinated with for centuries.

The closest planet, the reachable world.

A possible new land to colonize. Could life be supported?

But Mars is not the answer.

The star retreated, and Jeremiah was pulled along with it. And within a fleeting moment, the red planet was gone, lost in the heavens. As Jeremiah focused on the star, which kept him close, he looked outward into the heavens, and the surrounding stars passed at such a ferocious intensity and speed that he covered his face with his arms. Until he stopped suddenly, and Jeremiah opened his eyes.

Jupiter.

There was something awe-inspiring about the behemoth gas giant; the multicolored pastel gas clouds which raced across the top of the atmosphere; thirty miles thick, billowing, puffy, like balls of cotton, but still, nothing like he had ever seen on Earth.

For if he were to fall into the clouds of Jupiter, he would fall, and keep falling, until he reached the icy core through countless oblivions of racing gases and ferocious, deadly winds.

"Do you intend to take me to every planet?"

The star did not answer, but waited.

The white, hot pulsating plasma swirled in the sphere, as if mocking him, but then, Jeremiah finally listened.

The key is here.

Jeremiah paused, levitating in the midst of the galaxy, with the pastel beauty of the gas giant

Jupiter in plain sight before him, and looked over at the star.

"What is the key? Why have you taken me here?"

The star retreated back, disappearing around the side of Jupiter, and shot into space.

Jupiter is the key…

Jeremiah floated in front of Jupiter, motionless. He had never felt so alone. He did not say a word, for there was no one to talk to. He lay back, as he listened to the silence of space, and considered what the star told him.

Jupiter is the key.

The swirling gases spanned the giant sphere; angry pastels fought their way against one another.

Was Jupiter the key?

The surface-less gas giant?

The hostile planet of unbreathable atmospheres. Crushing gravitational pull. Perhaps a moon? Maybe Io or Titan?

Could one of those moons be the answer? Could it be found underneath the frozen ocean?

Clearly there was no way that Jupiter itself could be the answer to mankind's future existence…could it?

The first thing that Jeremiah could recall was the assault of the bright, hot lights as he struggled to open his eyes.

They were gritty.

And his eyelids felt heavy.

And his head.

He slowly raised his arms and placed his hands on his head. He grunted and closed his eyes again.

"The headache will pass," a familiar male voice said. "It's a normal side effect of this procedure. Expect it to last a few hours. You will want to remain in bed for that time. The headache can get pretty crippling."

He groaned and exhaled.

It was Cane.

That's who it was.

He kept his eyes closed and tried to lift his right arm, bringing it up to his throat.

"The sore throat too," Cane said. "Another side effect. Nurse Miranda here is bringing you some oral rehydration salts. It's a white powder. We mix it with water and you can sip on the solution, which will help you feel better. The procedure you experienced dehydrates you quite severely."

"You...could have warned me."

"It wouldn't have mattered. It's a procedure that we must perform on all new arrivals. These are unfortunate side effects, but they are temporary and you will return to normal within time."

Jeremiah slowly opened his eyes, and saw Cane standing over the bed. He looked down and smiled; Jeremiah noticed a missing tooth. But Jeremiah remained motionless and silent.

"So I am glad you are awake, but I am going to give you some time to rest, and later, when you are feeling better, we will meet again to review the results of your examination. Quite interesting, Mr. Walter. I honestly don't think that we have had examination results quite like yours ever before."

Jeremiah struggled to swallow and croaked. "Like…mine?"

Cane smiled and nodded as retreated towards the door.

"Yes, like yours. You have a very, very interesting mind Mr. Jeremiah. You will make an interesting addition to this colony. Welcome aboard."

Jeremiah looked up and over at Cane as he left, as he struggled to stay awake.

He tried to stay awake but lost, and he slept again.

Jeremiah hadn't remembered when he had been transferred.

It was as if a large portion of his memory was missing.

He opened his eyes slowly.

He was no longer inside the medical examination room, but in a small, modest chamber. It was furnished simply with a bed, and across from where he was lying, were several dressers lined against the wall.

His head was still pounding, and his eyes still felt heavy. There was a tube inserted into his mouth, he could feel a warm liquid running down the back of his throat.

A nurse entered the room, stood over his bed, looked down, and smiled. "I'm Nurse Miranda. You met me back in ME 1, though you may not remember me. But I see we are awake now."

The nurse moved about the room straightening pillows and blankets, as Jeremiah watched her movements. She wore a white uniform, and her red hair was cropped tight under a standard medical cap. She paused while folding a white sheet and looked over at him, and smiled. "There's a note pad on the bedside table. You can use it if you have any questions."

He turned his head towards the right and saw a plain, white pad – about six inches in length and two or three inches wide, with a small pen. He reached out for it and managed to drag the pen and paper over onto the bed.

Nurse Miranda set the sheets she had been folding on a nearby chair and stood by the side of the bed, looking down at the pad and pen, and then up at Jeremiah. She raised her eyebrows, as he started to scribble a few words.

I feel worse.

She smiled and looked down at him.

"You lost a lot of nutrients, Jeremiah. That's why we placed a feeding tube in your esophagus. But that should only be there for another 12 or 24 hours, and then it will be able to come out, and you'll be able to speak again."

Jeremiah fiddled with the pen in his right hand and scribbled again.

Where am I?

"These are your quarters," she said as she returned to the chair and her pile of folded sheets.

"I see from the monitors that your vitals are fine, and once you have reached normal levels with your rehydration and nutrients, Elder Cane will visit you and the results of your examination will be discussed. Until then, rest up, Jeremiah. You'll need your energy in the coming days."

She smiled and left. Jeremiah heard the hydraulics and the deep thud of the lock engaging.

He looked around the room again. It was a tiny, windowless room. It was just as cold and uninviting as the hallways had been when he and Cane walked towards the medical facility, and this room was no different. And then he fell asleep again.

Jeremiah opened his eyes, and the room was dark. How long had he been out?

He let his eyes adjust to the darkness, and he saw the small dresser off to the left. When he craned his neck around, he could see a bit of light finding its way inside from underneath the door.

He gasped and brought his hands up to his neck.

"Ba – ba – ba…"

His voice sounded unfamiliar against the silence of the room. But it was there. A bit raspy, but still there.

And the tube was gone.

Moments later, he heard a key and the click of a lock.

He heard the door open over to the side, and a few moments later, stark overhead lights illuminated and he saw Cane appear.

The man nodded and smoothed his silvery hair.

He took a breath. "The feeding tube was standard," he said. "Don't worry about that. We were just replacing your lost nutrients, Jeremiah. Are you feeling much better now? You've been sleeping for several days."

"Throat still hurts," he croaked.

"The tube will cause some irritation. Nothing to be alarmed about. But you are looking much better. The other day you had some pretty big bags under your eyes. But the procedure can be draining. Do you have the energy to sit up?"

Jeremiah looked down at his body, covered in a thin, white blanket. He nodded, and drew his arms up, placing his palms flat on the bed. He looked up at Cane and raised his eyebrows.

"Your strength will return in time. It' a draining process."

Jeremiah nodded and flopped back onto his pillow. He turned his head and looked at Cane. "So you're alone?"

Cane smiled. He turned around and grabbed a small, wooden chair from the opposite wall and slid it next to the bed. He sat and placed his arms on the side of the bed. "So," he said. "Tell me about your experience, Jeremiah."

Jeremiah looked down at his plate of vegetables. The plate was colorful; the mixture of bright orange carrots and squash intermingled with purple eggplant and brilliant green broccoli. They had a sufficient farming system set with artificial sunlight in the lower levels, so produce grew easily once watered. The misting system had worked for some time – until the water levels lowered – and, in the arid climate aboveground, there were few avenues of replenishment.

Still, the colorful plate of vegetables was not the type of food he had been used to in years past. He remembered when his plate had meat on it. Not any longer. Livestock was at its lowest level since the colonists had arrived in the catacombs, as they failed to reproduce.

When he looked back up around the room, he wondered when he might see his family again.

He remembered the days, growing up in the north, when life had been so much easier. When the sun had only shined for a few days, and when the air had still been breathable.

It was during those days, when he still lived in New Jersey, before the shift, which he remembered.

He remembered visiting the beaches on the Jersey shore, when the water would get closer towards the streets with each passing day. When the sea levels would rise, almost before his eyes. And eventually, year after year, the water engulfed all of the barrier islands, and rose further. And over the following years, the water levels would rise and completely submerge all of the buildings that had once risen from the waters that had covered the barrier islands years before, and then started to swallow the buildings on the mainland.

And that is when his family moved south, when the news had been talking about the oceans shifting.

They had heard, back in those years, of the cities down south – how New Orleans had become dry and sandy, how the marshes had dried up, with dusty leaves. And how all the crocodiles had died from the lack of water. And Miami – he had heard about that city too. How the everglades had dried up. How all of the wildlife had died, or flew away. And how the ocean just…left.

He remembered yelling at the newscasters as they did not have the answers.

"What do you mean the ocean just left? Where the heck did it go?" There had been so many questions, in his youth, when the television newscasts had become increasingly unbelievable.

"The ocean faded away to sand and the continental shelf, right?" Jeremiah had tried to remember, long and hard, about who had said that to him.

And then, he looked over at Cane, and understood.

As Jeremiah pushed the vegetables around his plate, he reached for a slice of bread, and tore it apart. As he chewed, he remembered the first day his family arrived at the catacombs.

A woman with dirty, stringy hair leaned down towards his plate. "Care for more, Jere?"

He looked up at the woman. She smiled and raised her eyebrows.

"I would rather some meat," he said, returning to his plate.

But now, he was sitting underground, in Florida, staring at a plate of bland vegetables because that's all there was.

The cattle were gone.

The cities in the north were flooded.

And life was now was so very, very different.

But it was a new kind of different.

It was the new normal, and the new normal was exactly what he wanted to escape. After a few minutes of moving his bland vegetables around his plate with his fork, he looked up and over at Elder Cane. The old man was engaged in a conversation with several other of the Elders.

"I would like to volunteer to go."

The table continued its chatter, but Elder Cane turned around and looked over at Jeremiah. The two made eye contact, and held it for a moment as the chatter around them continued.

After a few minutes, Elder Cane raised his arm up, and the room quickly silenced.

"What did you say Jeremiah?"

The conversation in the dining room quieted.

All of the eyes in the room focused on Jeremiah, who sat back and placed his hands in his lap, and looked directly at the Elder. "I was saying that I want to go. To find the habitable zone. I want to be the leader of the mission."

"You want to go there? To take that risk? To search for a place that may not even exist?"

Jeremiah placed his napkin on the table, lowered his eyes, and stepped up and aside from the bench he had been sitting on. He looked back up at the Elder and scanned the room.

"We are running out of supplies," he said. Elder Cane stood back and crossed his arms. "Every one of us who remains here is a drain on our precious little resources. We cannot keep living here indefinitely. And the world outside is hostile."

Jeremiah walked to the center of the dining area as he continued. "We had meat…for a few months, right? And our water. It's almost gone, right? There's no water table here anymore. Do you remember the Florida of years ago? When basements were impossible because the water table was too high? Look around, everyone! We're *living* in a basement. In Miami, of all places. We need to find more resources. Or we are going to wither away and die."

Elder Cane raised his hands. "Now Jeremiah," he said. "We have to consider the risks."

"I *have* considered the risks. Do you remember the days when our city was on the ocean? When it was tropical and rainy? Now if you go outside, it's dry, hot and sandy. We don't even *know* how far the nearest beach is from us. It could be many miles for all we know."

Elder Cane looked directly at Jeremiah. "And you are suggesting we explore that? Wander into uncharted territory? Lands and terrain that have never been mapped?"

Jeremiah shook his head. "No. And I am not saying that we should all go. I am just saying that we send a team to investigate the rumor of this habitable zone. If this habitable zone truly exists, we need to find it. And soon."

The room erupted in chatter as Elder Cane looked directly at Jeremiah.

They held their stare, and Elder Cane raised his hands for a minute as the chatter died down. He looked around the room, and Jeremiah took his seat.

"Please listen. Everyone." Elder Cane walked towards the end of the long, rectangular table, and looked down at the dining survivors.

"The scout that has arrived is in quarantine quarters right now. I mentioned this the other day. If our estimations are correct, he will be there for another ten days. After that time, we will be able to interrogate him. But he arrived severely dehydrated and malnourished. So he is also under medical treatment at this time."

"So what can we do in the meantime?" Jeremiah asked, as all eyes directed towards him. "Do we just sit here for another ten days? How many more days' rations do we have?"

"Jeremiah, enough. Ladies and Gentlemen, enjoy the rest of your dinner. I will keep you all updated on the condition of the scout, and when we can interrogate him, I will give you the information swiftly." He turned and left the room and chatter among the survivors rose.

Jeremiah pursed his lips and looked down towards his plate of root vegetables. As he examined them closely, he saw that they were hardly what one would consider "premium" grade.

In fact, they were close to spoiling, but he knew that this is what he and the survivors had been accustomed to for many months now – he knew, deep in his soul, that the food rations were dwindling.

And the water rations were getting far scarcer.

When he looked around the room, and at the women in particular, he did not notice the laughter and the chatter. Instead, he noticed the water glasses. They were large and dirty, tall, Collins glasses.

Possibly used from a hotel in Miami. He remembered the days scavenging the city for supplies.

But the type of glasses was really secondary; for they only had, at most, a tiny sip of water.

And then he looked at everyone's hair.

Mussed, matted. There was a stench in the air, of uncleanliness.

"How much water do we still have?" Jeremiah asked. "We hardly have enough to drink, let alone keep ourselves and our surroundings clean."

The other Elders looked directly at Jeremiah. One tall man stood. "We will speak to the scout once his health has improved and he has cleared quarantine. And then, after that, you will have your answers. Until then, we expect you to remain cooperative with the society, or we will see that you are held in lockdown."

Jeremiah scoffed and returned to his plate.

He downed his slip of dirty water, and slammed his glass down on the table. He got up and left the room, as the other survivors looked on in silence.

Elder Cane returned to the dining room and locked eyes with Jeremiah.

He held his stare, and watched as Jeremiah left, and then return to his bench and focused on his dinner as the conversation and chatter in the room returned.

Cane sat again, looked over from above his plate and back at Jeremiah, who threw his head back in laughter.

Those brilliant white teeth. Perfectly formed features.

Cane scoffed.

"Hey Jere," he called over. Jeremiah looked over at Cane and his face grew solemn.

"Why don't you stop philandering with those women and get over to the medical lab? Don't you have something you should be taking care of?"

He looked back at Cane and shook his head. He tapped his fingers on the side of the door. "Do I?"

And then sighed, turned around, and headed out the door as Cane looked on.

Jeremiah leaned back against the cool cement wall in the adjoining hallway and closed his eyes.

He balled his fist and slammed it against the wall.

There was a time when Elder Cane had not reigned supreme in the catacombs. Jeremiah could remember it like it was yesterday. And he wasn't sure how the Elder got into power – save the fact that he was an Elder – but Jeremiah questioned Elder Cane's purpose for not wanting to arrange a mission to search for the habitable zone. Certainly it was there, wasn't it?

And then there was the scout.

A complete and unexpected surprise.

And why would a scout arrive, out of the blue, at their door, and at the brink of death?

Why would a man – a seemingly common human being – take the risk against the harshness of the atmosphere to visit their colony?

And then he felt a hand on his shoulder.

It was a light touch, warm and reassuring, quite gentle.

He opened his eyes.

He knew the woman; despite the lack of water in the survivors' society, she had managed to maintain a presentable look, her hair tied back neatly in a pony-tail appeared quite clean, considering the circumstances.

And her skin was smooth, flawless, and she smiled with brilliant white teeth.

But despite her physical features, he felt her warmth.

"Miranda," he said.

She kept her hand on his shoulder and tilted her head to the side. "Jeremiah. You stormed out of there. We all know that you have good intentions."

Jeremiah scoffed and laughed. "Does Cane?"

Her face shifted as her eyes fell to the floor. "Yes…I think he does. But you know our situation is dire, Jere. You know that we cannot afford an exploration mission, right? We simply don't have enough rations."

Jeremiah shook his head and looked down the hallway. It stretched for hundreds of yards, was lined with doors. And at the end of the hallway, there was a set of double steel doors. He knew where those doors led to.

"Don't go there," she warned. "Or you will be placed in quarantine as well."

Jeremiah looked at Miranda and she smiled. "Why don't you rejoin the others? There's going to be a social this evening, and I'm sure tomorrow morning Cane will be more reasonable."

Jeremiah shook his head and walked away. "I'm heading back to my quarters."

Miranda sighed.

Elder Cane walked at a rapid pace down the same hallway that Jeremiah and Miranda were in moments previously. He approached the double steel doors at the end of the hallway and fished a gleaming key from his pocket. He drilled the medical staff, calling through the glass. "Where is he?! Where did he go? Where was he taken?"

He stormed through the set of stainless steel doors, and two nurses were frantically rummaging through several sets of drawers under the countertops on the opposite end of the room. Elder Cane looked over towards the bed. The mussed sheets stood out bright and white against the harshness of the lights.

But there was no scout.

Cane stopped in his tracks.

His voice was stern and firm. "Miranda! Where is he? Where did he *go*?"

She stopped rummaging through the drawers and turned to face him. She stood straight and still, and clasped her hands in front of her waist.

She looked down. "We left for just a moment – gathered dinner – and then when we got back, he was gone."

"He was…*gone*…how do you explain that? He just simply vanished?" He looked at both nurses. Miranda remained still and leaned against the edge of the counter, her hands remained clasped, and she looked downwards. Her stark blonde hair caught the bright overhead lighting. The other nurse said nothing. She looked over at Cane. A look of concern washed over her face, as she bit her lower lip.

"Go get Jeremiah," Cane said.

Jeremiah joined the others.

"So the scout is gone?" Jeremiah asked, craning his neck towards ME1.

"They called me a few minutes ago," Cane said. He looked at Jeremiah with a scowl on his face. "Do you know anything about this?"

Jeremiah shook his head. It was time to decide who was going to go. Who would represent humanity in a now foreign world? "I haven't a clue where he could have gone, Desmond. But how could he have just left without anyone noticing?"

Miranda looked up at Jeremiah and Cane. "I have been here the entire time. I never heard any alarms. I entered ME1 to check on him, and he was gone."

Jeremiah stood in the threshold of the ME1 door and looked at the bed. The sheets were mussed. He walked over to the bed and placed his palm down on the blanket. Still warm.

"This just happened," he said as Miranda nodded.

Cane walked to the exit doors. "Jeremiah, come with me. We have to arrange a town hall. Call Counselor Abagail and have her arrange a party to search each level. There's no way he could have gone back outside now."

Jeremiah ran to catch up with Cane. "Don't you think we should decide who goes?"

"Maybe," Cane said. "First item of business: we need to find this scout. If he's off in the colony…" His voice trailed off as they walked towards the common areas.

They never found the scout.

After hours of searching the hallways, from the ground level and deep, down towards the basement levels, their search yielded nothing. Until Cane was paged, and notified that the scout was back in his room in ME1, and lying in bed, still in a coma.

"I'm liking this visitor less and less," Cane said, as they met Counselor Abagail in the receiving area. She stood tall and confident. Her red hair was tied back in a bun. "Cane, Jeremiah."

"Keep an eye on the scout," Cane said to Counselor Abagail. "Have two guards stationed outside ME1. Let me know when he wakes up."

Jeremiah and Cane opened the door to the amphitheater. The noise of multiple conversations wafted outside the room, as Counselor Abagail turned to leave. The two men walked inside and looked at each other. "Take a seat, Jeremiah. It's time to discuss our situation with the colony."

Jeremiah stood in the amphitheater and looked over at Elder Cane, who was looking back up at him. "Shall I go?" he called down to Cane. "How many times must I tell you that I am the best candidate?" Cane waved him away as Jeremiah found a seat. Cane navigated the steps down towards the presentation area. There was a small podium at one end of the room, and a large conference table on the other. The seats were filled with colonists.

Cane took the podium and addressed the colonists about the dire situation of their dwindling supplies and water. He had to speak over the noise.

The chatter in the room quieted.

All looked up towards the back of the theatre, and up at Jeremiah. "I have volunteered multiple times, dear Elder. I can go and get supplies."

Cane leaned back. "Do you have an idea – dear sir – of the inherent risks involved? Of what you can expect to find out there once you leave this compound?"

Jeremiah sat and the others returned their attention to Elder Cane, who stood down at the base of the amphitheater, in front of a large chalkboard. The lighting shined against his bald head.

"Ladies and gentlemen," he said. "I thank you for your interest in this expedition. But first and foremost, I must review the risks of the endeavor."

He started to remind the group of the shift of the seas. There were a significant amount of volunteers who did not understand that grand event.

As Cane spoke, Jeremiah remembered.

He had still been a child, but he remembered the days in New Jersey, packing up the family car with everything they could carry, and leaving the state.

He could still remember standing in the kitchen, just a small boy at the time, holding his teddy bear and blanket. He watched his mother and father rush through the house, carrying boxes, trash bags filled with clothes, and rolling suitcases. He could still hear the click-click of the wheels as they ran across the edges of the kitchen tiles.

He could still hear the emergency newscast on the television as his family scurried around the house. "The wave is traveling across the Atlantic Ocean at approximately 300 miles per hour. New Jersey will be completely inundated, along with the low lying areas of Pennsylvania, Delaware and Maryland. When the event has concluded, we expect the new northern USA coastline to be somewhere between North Carolina and Virginia. We urge all residents to seek higher ground immediately. Take only what you can."

The newscast stopped and Jeremiah had looked up at his father with wide eyes. "We'll be okay, Jere. We'll find a new place to live."

Jeremiah was brought back to the present after Cane questioned the colonists about who was interested in forming a supply expedition. Jeremiah raised his hand instantly.

Later that night, Jeremiah lay back in his bunk and closed his eyes, placing his hands behind his head. As soon as he did, thoughts of the days before the catacombs entered his mind.

He couldn't stop thinking about packing up in New Jersey as the ocean made its way closer to the houses, as it swallowed them up with each high tide. He had run through his house with his parents as the water lapped towards the front door.

"It's time to leave!" Father said.

Jeremiah slept fitfully that night.

As the daylight started to fade, a dusty sedan was parked on the side of a broken highway in the southeastern United States.

There were no other cars for miles.

But the new land, the new mega-continent that was forming, in some cases right before the survivors' eyes, blew hot sand across the deserted landscape.

The skyscrapers of Atlanta rose through the rising sands, as the driver of the car, a middle aged man, struggled to restart the engine as the right side of the vehicle was getting pounded with blowing sand.

"Hurry! Start it! What's wrong with it?!" A slightly younger blonde woman cried to the man, as he shook his head and wiped the sweat from his brow.

A baby wailed in the back seat.

"I'm trying, Norma!" he said. "Damn thing won't turn over!" He tapped the instrument panel. "I think the gas is just too low."

Norma's face shifted as her eyes widened. "What are we gonna do, Nelson? We have to get to Wichita. That's where the news said to go. We can't go back to Miami. We know that.

But we can't stay in Atlanta! Aren't they just as bad off?"

Nelson banged his hands against the steering wheel. "Dammit, Norma! Let me think! Give me a minute."

Nelson shook his head and reached for the radio, finding only static. He remembered, not long ago, when things had been better. When Miami had not been so far from the sea. When the air had been breathable, and when the sunlight had not been deadly.

But those days were now in a newly distant past. For he knew, that if his family got out of the car, and even attempted to find gas, or even walk to Atlanta, that they would be burned by the sun within minutes.

He sat back in his seat as the baby wailed on, his hand curled into a fist, resting against his mouth. He looked out the window at the shriveled trees and blowing sand.

After a few minutes, he looked over at Norma, who had reached into the backseat and gotten little Gabby out of her car seat.

"We have to go to Miami," he said, looking down at Norma as she coddled the baby. "They have the best facility. I can leave you there. But I won't stay."

Norma looked up. "Why not? You won't stay?"

Nelson leaned back, paused, and looked over at Norma. She started to nurse the baby and looked up at Nelson expectantly. He shrugged and waited a few minutes. "We both know why we came here," he said. "I knew this was going to happen. Knew all along. They didn't. The dumb fucks. But what can you expect? They wouldn't know anyway."

"So what do we do, then? We're subject to the same turmoil, as you can see."

Nelson nodded slowly and sat back in the driver's seat. "Yes. Yes, I know." He looked out the window at the empty terrain and waited a few minutes. He listened to the rustling of Norma's clothing as she finished nursing the baby.

He continued looking out the driver's side window as he listened to Norma's rustling, moving through the cabin of the car, placing the baby in the backseat, and when he heard her thump against the passenger seat, he turned around. "We'll go to Miami," he said. "They're the strongest colony. I can convince them. But you will need to come later."

"Come later?"

He pursed his lips. "Well…you'll have to wait until they find you. If I'm going to approach them alone."

The scout had been an unexpected visitor.

And the survivors, who had been used to months, even years of silence, of looking through windows, upwards towards a now foreign land, were taken aback when they first saw his approach, out of the blue, while the sun was still shining; it was a terrain which was filled with unbreathable air; a relentless sun that shined all hours of the day, for months at a time, and skeletons from the past – both made of bone but also made of steel.

When the scout was spotted, he was walking towards their outer portal, from the city, in a haphazard, and drunken manner. He had been unsteady on his feet, and clutched a gas mask over his face, holding it, as he nearly fell, was covered in dirt, and finally spilled to the ground, just at the entrance. He held his arms up as his mask fell to the ground.

His face was so dirty, his features had become undiscernible.

The whites of his teeth gleamed against the sunlight, as his hair matted on the sides of his face, running with sweat and dirt, forming a roadmap down his cheeks.

He tried to speak but could not.

A watchman who was standing and looking out the window, and who had watched the visitor approach, looked back towards the others when he saw the visitor collapse. "Counselor! Do we venture outside and rescue him?"

A large redheaded woman stood and joined the watchman at the window. She saw the mysterious man, laying on the ground just outside, now motionless.

"Counselor Abagail? What should we do?"

She nodded.

The watchman joined two other men who started to put on their masks and radiation suits.

They looked over at Counselor Abagail. She nodded again and retreated back towards the adjoining room, and tied a white cloth over her nose and mouth.

"Go, bring him in," she said, her voice now muffled and quivered. "Get him inside."

PART THREE

THE MESSAGE

Then I saw "a new heaven and a new earth," – for the first heaven and the first earth had passed away, and there was no longer any sea   (21:1 KJV)

There will be the day where the heavens will become an Earth and the Earth will become heavens. – REVELATIONS

ELI DE JESUS STOOD outside of medical. He paced in front of the steel double doors, every so often pausing and looking through the small, square windows that were roughly one third of the way down from the ceiling. He saw a few nurses scurrying through the examination room, and in and out of ME 1. He had a feeling about who the visitor was.

He leaned against the cool cement wall and closed his eyes. He'd been just a teenager when he had first seen the man. Still in high school. When he first saw the man, he had thought nothing of it. But he could still remember back a couple of decades. When the man visited him in the school. In fact, he visited the entire school in a special auditorium session where the entire student body had gathered to listen to the man speak.

And as Eli sat in the back row, fiddling with his pen, writing in the wide ruled notebook his mother gave him, he paused as he heard the voice in the front of the auditorium, and raised his head as he started to listen.

"Do you know what is going to happen? What's about to inflict this world in the coming decades?"

Eli looked around the room, but the student body remained silent. He looked towards the front, and saw the man, looking out at the audience. His hands were on his hips. "Is anyone listening to me?"

A few hands raised as the man pointed to one student who stood. "You are a scientist, right?"

The man nodded. "Yes. My name is Nelson Moses. I've been traveling throughout the world – not only in the United States – and giving these lectures on the fate of the planet." He looked back out at the students as the one boy sat down. "I can tell you what's about to happen. It's on a global scale. And it will change the world as you know it."

Back in the present, Eli opened his eyes, and shook his head.

He turned around and looked back through the small window, over towards ME 1. There was something about this scout. He looked far too familiar.

But Eli did not always trust his mind. Nor his sense of intuition. And there had been times that he had failed his own self.

He had remembered the sunlight, as it filtered into his bedroom. His arms and legs ached, and he turned and buried his face in the pillow. Long gone were the days of school, now he was a man, with his own house, and his own problems.

There was a knock on his bedroom door.

He wrapped the pillow on his head and a few moments of silence passed. And then the knock came again, this time louder; three raps on the hallowed wood frame. "Eli, now! It's time to go now! Wake up!"

And he heard the footsteps trail down the hallway away from his bedroom door. He sat up and flung the pillow to the side of the bed, and rubbed his palms over his eyes. It couldn't be time yet. There just hadn't been any time.

He opened his eyes and looked over towards the window. The sun was shining just as brilliantly as it had before. No changes. The crosshatch network of shadows from the windowpane remained on the floor, the small squares of sunlight looked like small, yellow boxes.

Winston had been correct. Hadn't he?

As Eli sat on the bed, now deep in thought, it took every sliver of energy that still coursed through his body – the freight train that he believed hit him had long since left the station – but he continued to feel the after effects of the days before.

The newscasts had said to leave weeks ago, but they remained.

The last of the cars had left the streets and pulled away. Most headed south.

And then Winston burst through his bedroom door. Eli shifted his face and pulled the sheet over his shirtless torso. "Don't you knock!?"

Winston held onto the doorframe and paused for a moment to catch his breath.

"It's coming!" He lunged forward towards the bed and grabbed Eli's arm, and yanked. "We have to go! Now!"

Eli knew what Winston was talking about, and bolted out of bed and towards the dresser and fished some jeans out of a drawer. He hopped on one leg as he looked up at Winston. "How much time to do you think we have?"

"Less than an hour! Let's go!" Winston pulled Eli into the hallway, looking back at him as they navigated the hallway. "I tried to wake you up all night! The sirens have been going off for hours now."

But Eli wasn't listening to Winston. He was listening to what sounded like running water. He stopped.

Winston turned around and held his arms up. "What?!"

Eli initially looked up towards the ceiling. He then looked down the hallway; it was the same hallway lined with bedroom doors that he and Winston had shared together, in the four bedroom house in the outer suburbs of Philadelphia, it was a brick colonial. They both fell in love with the spring cherry blossoms and the equally brilliant fall foliage. But now, over a decade later, he thought this moment would be the last moment he would ever stand in his upstairs hallway.

"What is it, Eli?"

After scanning the upstairs foyer and looking down the lengthy hallway, Eli rested his eyes on Winston. He smiled. Eli thought, just for a fleeting moment, that despite their different backgrounds – Winston being from the American South – with a penchant for "soul food" and equally soulful music; Eli from Miami.

Eli loved the contrast in their skin tones, and cherished the differences in their culture. He looked directly at Winston and took a deep breath. "Stop and listen to me."

Winston leaned in closer, as the running water sounded louder. He leaned in towards Eli's ear, and did not shout; he spoke in a clear and distinct voice, very matter of fact: "You know I love you more than the world itself. And I know you don't want to lose this house."

Eli started to turn his head and Winston gently placed his hand on Eli's chin and prevented him from doing so. "By mid-morning, this house will be gone. Gone. So let's get out of here!"

"Oh, fuck." Eli hung his head down.

Winston nodded and placed his arm around Eli's shoulder. "It's just nails and wood, hon. Insulation." Eli looked over at the doors as Winston slowly started walking him to the other end of the hallway; the first door they passed had been their office. He remembered many days sitting there, at the giant desk in the center of the room, staring at the computer and browsing through scores of old photos.

"Just forget it, Eli. It's all going to be underwater before noon. We must go. Come with me."

Eli slowly turned away from the door. "Our memories…"

Winston forced him further down the hallway, but gently so, with a pillow touch. "It's the memories. That's what we take with us. This house…it's just a bunch of building materials. Like a giant puzzle pieced together. But it's the memories that we take with us. Not the house. Or the things."

And Winston led him down the stairs, as the flowing, dark, grey seawater flowed from the east side of the house – back towards the kitchen – to the west side of the house, out through the living room windows and into the front yard. Within minutes, the water level had risen from just a few inches to over a foot. And the waves were continuing their surge.

"The surge is coming fast," Winston said. Eli looked at the water, watching the furniture float around the living room. His art journals were floating through the water, washing back and forth from the dining room to the front wall in the living room. He recognized their colorful artwork. He looked up at Winston. "How are we going to get out of here?"

Years later, in the catacombs, Eli leaned against the wall and started removing his radiation suit, just after the scout had been brought inside. He took a deep breath, closed his eyes, and shook his head.

Counselor Abagail looked on and stood over the others as they retrieved the mysterious visitor. Cane came running as the team pulled him inside. "Close the doors! Are you crazy? The atmosphere is too thin! And the radiation!"

Eli turned around. "The daylight is fading. It's almost time for the sun to set. Few more days at most, I think. And we don't know if there is radiation at lethal levels. He survived didn't he? Stop panicking." His voice sounded muffled through his helmet.

Counselor Abagail took a few steps away from the visitor, looked back at Eli, and then at the team. "Take him to medical and place him in quarantine. Go! Do it now!"

They dragged the man into the center of the floor as a team of medical personnel arrived with a gurney. His eyes were closed and he appeared unconscious.

After the call was received throughout the compound, others started to arrive. Jeremiah and Cane arrived together. Jeremiah was the first to approach, and placed his hand on Counselor Abagail's shoulder. "Counselor, what is this? A stranded warrior?"

She shook her head. "De Jesus spotted him. Through the window. He was coming up towards the doors from the city. But I don't think he will survive much longer. Just look at his skin."

Jeremiah knelt down beside the visitor. He looked down at the mysterious man, who was now clearly unconscious, his eyes closed and his mouth was open.

"Take him now. And use the protective gear," Elder Cane said.

A team assembled and gathered equipment in the adjoining room as some kneeled close to the man who seemed to scarcely hold onto life.

Eli followed with a gurney and handed out masks as the others hovered over the mysterious visitor, who lay motionless, yet breathing, eyes closed and unresponsive.

Counselor Abagail stood and motioned for Eli to come closer. He rolled the gurney next to the body as the others stood and took a few steps away to clear the area.

"Put him on the gurney," she said.

Miranda and Caterina stood and watched as Eli knelt down next to the body. He looked up at

Counselor Abagail. "How do we know…that he isn't virulent?"

"We don't," she said. "We are taking him straight to quarantine."

The man looked burned.

Severely so – his skin was brilliant red; cooked. Blackened in some places. He was huddled on the floor and his breathing was labored. He didn't look up at the others, he simply rested his head on the floor and closed his eyes.

Caterina stood with Cane and the Counselor. "Didn't he know about the sun? That it's too hot this time of year?"

Counselor Abagail shook her head as the visitor was covered in plastic. A man dressed in white handed her a small ring which she scanned on her wrist and handed back. "Just get him into quarantine," she said to the man dressed in white. "Immediately. We don't know if he has some new, unfounded disease that could run rampant through the colony. Or radiation poisoning. If he survives, we will interview him. Certainly he has some sort of purpose for coming here."

Eli paused after removing his helmet. He looked over at Counselor Abagail. "I think I have seen him before. He looks oddly familiar."

Jeremiah paused and looked up and over at Eli. "What do you mean? You know this man?"

Eli stepped out of his suit and took a cautious step forward as he shrugged his shoulders. He looked over at Jeremiah, and then the Counselor, and back at Jeremiah. "I – well – don't know for sure."

Jeremiah nodded. "What do you know, Eli?"

He looked down and exhaled. "I don't know for sure," he said. "I mean…his face…he has so many injuries and burns. But he looks so familiar. Like I have seen him before!"

Jeremiah studied a clipboard, lifting the pages slowly. "Do you have a specific memory? One that is making you feel this way?"

Eli raised his eyes and looked up at Jeremiah. "Do you remember that guy who was going around and lecturing before the wave came? I mean, we were both still teenagers then. But do you remember? I think his name was Moses."

Jeremiah bit his lip and cocked his head to the side. He shook his head.

"I swear, Jere. I've seen that guy before. I remember when it was all over the news – back before the shift. When that guy traveled across the country and had that lecture series…do you remember, Jere?"

Jeremiah paused and looked down at the scout as Eli waved his hand in front of Jeremiah's face. "You in a trance?"

Jeremiah caught himself and looked up. "Uh, no….I…"

"What were you thinking about?"

Jeremiah paused and took a breath. "This man…I mean…hearing what you were saying jogged my memory. He looks familiar to me as well."

"So you saw him when he was going around telling everyone the wave was coming? That the world was going to end?"

Jeremiah shook his head. "No, that's not where I saw him."

"Then where was it then?"

"I'm not sure…"

Eli looked over at Jeremiah who busied himself helping the others bring the scout to medical quarantine. There was something odd about Jeremiah's claim. If he didn't see this man traveling the country – and the world – before the wave came, where had he seen him?

Medical Exam Room 1 (ME1) was beyond the double doors on the other side of the entry chamber to triage.

Miranda assisted Jeremiah as they hoisted the visitor onto the bed and covered the bed with an expansive, clear bubble. She reached for a long, translucent cord and attached it to a large, plastic clear bubble as several monitors awakened, instantly displaying vital information.

Counselor Abagail joined the others in ME 1. "Well, his vitals are stable," she said. She looked down at the visitor. "He seems to be in a coma…or…"

"Or what?" Cane entered the room and placed his hands on his hips and looked directly at Counselor Abagail. "Do you think he is carrying some sort of a virus?"

She looked down and shook her head. "There are so many vastly different species outside now – even since we came here – that it's quite possible he could have an illness for which we do not have immunity. Even something as simple as a cold."

Eli and Miranda stood and looked on.

"So we keep him in quarantine," Cane said, without hesitation. "At least until he wakes up from this coma, or whatever it is. I don't know what his intentions are. Or what reason he had for traveling in the sun. No wonder he is covered with so many burns."

Miranda looked up and over at Cane and Counselor Abagail. "Would you like me to treat his burns?"

They both nodded. "And nourish him," Cane said. "See that he is hydrated. We don't turn others away here. But get security detail on this room. I don't know what his intentions are." Cane held the door as he spoke. "And let me know the instant he wakes up."

Cane left ME 1 and let the door close behind him. He shook his head as he continued down the south corridor. This hadn't been the first time that a mysterious visitor had appeared at the colony, and it most likely would not be the last. The first visitor had been hostile, and back in those days, he had been far more inviting.

Not this time.

This visitor had to give good reason for appearing at their doorstep.

A pretty damn good reason.

There was once a time that they knew the earth. When they knew her; the planet they grew up upon.

She had been a loving caregiver.

Her oceans had provided water and sea life; the plains had provided food, a means for growing more food, and the supplies for shelter.

But now, as Jeremiah looked outwards into the city, from the window of the outer portal, it all seemed so different.

The skyscrapers were still there, as they had been standing there for years, but once the sun would set, the view would be complete darkness for six months. No lights of the city. No glow reflecting against the night sky.

Just a dark skeleton.

He started down the hallway, returning to his quarters, when he saw Cane in the distance. "Cane!" he called, running towards the man.

Cane looked down and signed a few documents and then gave it to the staff member.

"What is it?" He started towards the offices, as Jeremiah followed.

"I wanted to speak to you about this visitor," he said. "Do you have a few minutes?"

Cane stopped and looked Jeremiah directly in the eyes. "Look. You were all over this one. Keep this as your baby. You've been asking for more. This is more. I have other things to worry about." Cane turned to leave but Jeremiah grabbed his arm.

Cane looked down at Jeremiah's hand and then up into his eyes, dumbfounded. Jeremiah removed his hand.

"Sorry," he said.

Cane nodded. "I would imagine so. Now what is it? I have a meeting in just a few minutes."

Jeremiah took a deep breath, and then made eye contact with Cane. "I have my reservations about this visitor. This scout."

Cane scoffed as his face shifted. "You can't handle this?"

Jeremiah nodded. "I can handle these type of things, Cane, but this is bigger than this colony. I need you in on this."

"In on what?"

Jeremiah placed his hand on Cane's shoulder and maintained eye contact with him. "Eli approached me a while ago. But he told me that he has seen this guy before."

Cane shook his head. "And how is that possible? Eli has been venturing outside without our knowledge?"

Jeremiah shook his head. "No, I think it goes much deeper than that."

Cane ushered Jeremiah in a nearby conference room and they shut the door. Cane pulled out two chairs and they sat down at the table next to each other. Cane paused and looked Jeremiah in the eyes. Jeremiah hadn't remembered the man getting so close before. His eyes were wide open. His face shifted. And Jeremiah could smell the man's deodorant. Cane looked away and slammed his wrists down on the table. "What the hell is this Jere? What is this? Some way that you're trying to stir the pot?"

Jeremiah raised his hands, palms open. "No, Cane. Not at all. I'm dead serious."

"So what is it then? What is going on that you need me in on?"

Jeremiah looked down and took a breath. "So Eli says he has seen this man before."

Cane nodded. "Yes."

"And even though this scout is pretty banged up, Eli said that it's the same guy who spoke at his high school…decades ago. Guy named Moses. Nelson Moses?"

Cane looked up at Jeremiah. "What? You're kidding me."

Jeremiah shook his head.

"So how will he know for sure?"

"Well, the scout is in quarantine. They're concerned about radiation and viruses."

Cane nodded as Jeremiah continued. "And Eli doesn't have ME access anyway. So he's going to have to wait until the quarantine lifts and this scout is allowed to intermingle with the population – if ever."

Cane asked: "So you're saying he can't confirm if he has seen this guy before or not?"

Jeremiah shook his head. "Not right now. I've ordered quarantine on the guy. And after that, we need to question him. In detail."

"And what about after that? Do you have a plan?"

Jeremiah leaned back in the chair and looked down for a moment, and then back up at Cane. "Well. I don't know yet. There are too many unanswered questions here."

He leaned forward, closer to Cane. "What if he is hostile? How will we protect the colonists?"

Cane leaned back and smiled. "And those are good questions to ask, Jere. I'm glad to see you are starting to think like a leader."

Word had traveled through the colony about the mission to find the habitable zone. After the town hall in the amphitheater, there were others who sought to join the mission.

Not long after the town hall, Jeremiah stood in the hallway outside the conference rooms. He looked through the windows. It had turned dark. He looked out towards the darkness outside, his view from a long, rectangular window, which was one of many long, rectangular windows, which spanned the length of the hallway, protecting from the harmful rays during daylight, but preventing a claustrophobic feel like on the lower levels.

He looked at the skeleton of the city in the distance, barely making out the dark structures against the night sky.

And on nights like this, the skyscrapers would sometimes be visible, against the blue light of the moon, but never the lighted and vibrant buildings that once had been…at least before the oceans shifted toward the poles.

Miranda joined him and placed her hand on his shoulder.

"Are you ready, Jere?"

He turned around and saw her warm smile. Jeremiah looked into her eyes. "Are you sure you want to come with me? We might never return, you know. This habitable zone may not even exist. It could just be a rumor."

Miranda nodded and looked downwards. "You already know the answer to that question." She looked back up at Jeremiah.

He took a deep breath, and turned around to face the group in Conference B.

There were several others who had the courage to join them and search for the habitable zone, and they each sat around a long, expansive steel table.

Miranda was the first to sign up once the request went to the group of survivors after the dinner gathering just a few short days after the scout had arrived. She leaned against the outer wall, next to the door, holding her gear at her side, and holding her gas mask in her other hand.

"I'm sure, Jere," she said, picking up her backpack and hoisting it over her shoulder. She looked at the others. "If we won't go, who will? And if no one goes, how will we all survive?"

Jeremiah nodded, looked around the room, and scanned the others.

Next to Miranda was Winston. Another early arrival.

He had been part of the colony since its inception; a native resident of Philadelphia, he was a founder of their colony along with Elder Cane. And after the oceans retreated from the Miami area and the water table dried up, he was one of the first survivors to search for any type of underground shelter, which had led to the discovery of the catacombs.

The last one to join to the group was Eli.

It had taken quite a bit of convincing to get him to come along.

Jeremiah remembered a night the previous week, as the four sat inside his quarters, when Eli shook his head. "It's just too dangerous," he said. "The air is hardly breathable. And even if you can breathe, we have no way to navigate. Maps are useless. We have no idea what this new continent will bring. And the winds blow sand at the strength of a hurricane…"

Jeremiah held his hands up as the group all looked up and focused on him. "I don't think it's quite that bad, guys. We will coordinate our departure soon, since it's the start of dark season," he said. "And the winds…yes…we will have to deal with them. Miranda, do you have any ideas to protect ourselves from the winds?"

She cleared her throat. "Well, we do have the ROVERS in the parking garages just above ground. And there is some extra fuel stockpiled. So we could drive. That should help. But it can't be the entire trip. I don't even know what we are going to face out there. I haven't been outside the catacombs since…"

Jeremiah looked over at Eli who raised his eyebrows. "It's a risk," Jeremiah said. "We all understand it, Eli."

"What about provisions?" Eli asked, folding his arms in front of his chest.

Eli didn't get a chance to answer when Elder Cane appeared through the set of double steel doors. All heads turned and eyes focused on him.

"That is why I said that this is a mission of the highest risk," he said, joining the group. "And if you wait a few minutes to leave, you will see that I will bring us adequate provisions – I hope, at least – for the journey."

Jeremiah stood back and looked up at Elder Cane. They left Conference B towards Bay 1, where Counselor Abagail was waiting with several others in security detail. Cane was dressed for the outdoors. He wore the same grey outerwear that the rest of the group had been wearing.

"A change of heart?" Miranda asked Cane.

Elder Cane walked over to the panel next to the outer portal. "What do you have the settings placed to?" He looked over at Jeremiah. "You know that this door self-closes once we leave. But there is a time delay. You need to leave it under one minute. And it's set to five minutes. If anyone were to come in here after we left, they might suffocate. Atmosphere's too thin." He shot a glance over at Jeremiah, and the others could sense a projection of disapproval coming from the Elder.

Counselor Abagail joined him at the panel. "Time delay, 2 minutes. The inner doors will close before the outer doors open."

Cane nodded as Counselor Abagail headed towards the inner corridor. "We will keep a close monitor of you and all of your vitals from Bay 3."

She turned and looked back at the group. "God's speed to you all."

And she headed down the corridor.

Jeremiah walked over to Elder Cane and tapped him on his shoulder, and walked towards the side room where the expedition gear was hanging on the wall.

Jeremiah leaned in close towards Elder Cane's ear. "Elder," he said. "You have been doubting this mission from the start. Are you now questioning my capability for leading this team?"

Elder Cane shook his head, looked over at the others, who were quietly keeping to themselves. The others kept busy, rummaging through the supplies in the entry area and prepping a hovering pallet in the center of the bay.

"A small oversight like the improper settings for the door can cost lives," he said. "And *despite* our lack of supplies, the society cannot afford a loss of life."

Jeremiah walked up to Cane and stood in front of him. Cane looked up, and then stood in front of Jeremiah. "You can't go Elder. Like you said, the mission is of the highest risk. We may not return. The colony can't afford to lose us both."

Cane glared at Jeremiah as everyone put their atmospheric masks on. Cane's voice sounded muffled as he spoke through his viewfinder. "Son, I am the leader of this colony. And if we are going to take a red mission, I am going to ensure that it is successful."

As the crew stood in the center of Bay 1, Counselor Abagail watched from the monitors in Bay 2.

Cane, Jeremiah. Eli and Winston. And Miranda for her medical expertise.

They stood next to the hovering pallet, stocked to its maximum weight with supplies.

"It's just fifty yards or so to the vehicles," Jeremiah said. "We'll head that direction and grab ROVER 1."

They nodded.

Jeremiah looked over at Cane, who raised his eyebrows. Miranda and Eli stood and fidgeted. Jeremiah looked over at Cane one last time. He nodded again.

Jeremiah turned towards the camera and gave a thumbs up.

The hydraulics hissed behind them as an anonymous woman announced sternly over the P.A. in a robotic voice –

INTERIOR PORTAL CLOSING.

They each looked back at the closing door, and then at each other.

Despite the thickness of the helmet viewfinders, they could clearly see one another's eyes. And as they were sealed off from the colony, the small group of five were isolated and stood, waiting, for the outer door to open.

The door which would lead to the unknown; to areas once beloved and inviting, now were hostile and unexplored. They each looked at the outer portal as several alarms sounded, and red lights flashed up and down the exterior walls as the P.A. repeated the audible announcement –

WARNING! WARNING!

EXTERIOR PORTAL OPENING!

Eᴌɪ ʟᴏᴏᴋᴇᴅ ᴏᴜᴛ ᴏғ ᴛʜᴇ

WINDOW as he had stood guard in the entry chamber, shortly after the scout had arrived to Sector B. The night was silent and still, and he looked upwards towards the sky, and tried to count the stars. He leaned his head against the glass, and treasured the cold feeling against his forehead.

He closed his eyes.

"Do you see Mars?"

Those had been the words of his father. Yes, he remembered. He remembered the night his father had set up the telescope. The big white one that he got for Christmas. Back when he was a child.

He remembered looking at the stars then. He had been under the same stars years before, when he was still a boy, when his father was still alive, standing above him, adjusting the telescope. He could still remember the crisp, clean scent of his father's antiperspirant.

And he remembered the stars. So many stars.

"I can't count them, Dad. I'm trying."

His father let out a chuckle, and took a breath, looking inside the tiny viewfinder, his face squinted. "There's billions and billions, Eli. Too many to count."

"Where's Mars?"

His father took a step back from the telescope, looking down at little Eli, and smiled.

"Here," he said, holding out his arms. "Let me lift you up. I'll show you."

And then, so many years later, Eli stood in the colony with his forehead pressed against the cool glass, and looked for Mars.

"There it is, isn't she a beauty?" His father held him up, and he looked in the little square viewfinder at the red planet, and he squealed. "Dad! I see it!" Eli snapped his head away from the telescope. "Is that really another...*planet*?"

Father nodded.

Eli leaned back and touched his hand to his forehead. It had started to get cold, and numb. And then he turned his head and looked back out at the horizon; he saw the millions of stars above; he looked out at the stars, watching the tiny, white orbs in the dark sky, blinking, watching and wishing.

And for the first time in years, he wished that his father were there with him.

Once the visitor was stabilized, Miranda hung back in ME 1 as the other medical personnel headed towards the conference room at the opposite end of the south corridor.

Cane walked fast and with determination, and the heels of his shoes click-clacked against the polished cement, and echoed against the barren walls. Counselor Abagail joined him.

"We must discuss this with the colony," he said. "Over dinner tonight I will let them know. What about Jeremiah? What all does he know about this visitor?"

Cane looked over at Counselor Abagail and she shook her head. "I don't know. I wasn't aware Jeremiah knew anything about him at all."

"Well, don't discuss anything about this with him yet. Let him discuss with the others, but not us. I don't need him meddling in this. He doesn't think things through, and with this situation, we need some circumspect."

Counselor Abagail nodded and looked at Cane as they paused in front of several giant steel doors.

The smell of cooking food permeated the air. Counselor Abagail placed her hand on Cane's shoulder. "Are you planning on arranging a team? To explore once the sun completely sets? I'm being told we are dangerously low on supplies. That an expedition needs to be arranged."

He held his hand up and nodded. "We are alright for now," he said. "We still have several weeks before sunset. A very tiny window. It's too dangerous out there. The sun rays have to be gone. And darkness. We need darkness. And with this visitor...I want to wait, Abby. For as long as we possibly can. We have to find out why that visitor targeted our facility, and what his purpose was for venturing out in the sunlight."

Counselor Abagail touched his arm lightly. "And we will venture out once the sun has cleared the horizon? The colonists need food, Desmond. We need to find sources of water. We are nearly dry. Even the farming zones are running dry. The crops are less and less."

Cane yanked his arm away. He knew the crops on the lower levels were withered. "Yes I am fully aware of that."

He opened the door to the dimly lit dining hall. It was filled with colonists and the dull roar of chatter.

He turned around and looked directly at Counselor Abagail.

"And yes. We will be arranging an expedition. But not until after we have spoken with the visitor. I will make the announcement tonight. And you – instruct your staff to keep him alive and nurse him back to health. We can't afford for him to die."

Cane disappeared into the dining hall as Counselor Abagail stood and watched the door close.

She knew how low their supplies were.

As second in command of the colony, she was fully aware of the day to day concerns of the colonists. And it was up to her to filter them from Cane. But this time, this month, their supplies had been particularly dwindled, and she knew that the usual gathering mission had to happen as soon as the sun cleared the horizon – or they were going to run out of potable water. She shook her head and sighed, as her assistant called for her. "Counselor, the visitor is stable. Miranda is still monitoring his condition and will notify us when he wakes."

She looked over at the young girl as she smiled, nodded her head and retreated. Couldn't have been more than twenty-five. Probably only knew this life.

Counselor Abagail nodded as Caterina skipped off, and then she gasped and remembered. Caterina had been one of the first colony babies. How could she have only known this purgatory?

Had they really been living down there already for a quarter of a century? Had it been that long? Counselor Abagail looked over at the window on the opposite end of the hallway; it was a tiny, rectangular view, but it offered some reassurance that they still lived on Earth —when the sun was shining, she would sometimes stand and look outside that very same window, and look to the past.

Everyone was surprised – humanity all across the planet – at how quickly the water receded from the south and the tropics and flooded the north and the poles. But now…it was a completely different world. The skyscrapers were crumbling and abandoned as the buildings of a once burgeoning downtown metropolis were being reclaimed by nature. She shook her head and snapped back to the present.

"Caterina!" she called down the hallway. Her voice echoed against the concrete walls.

She stopped skipping and walked back towards where Counselor Abagail stood. "Are you going to dinner?"

The young girl nodded and brushed her sandy, blonde hair away from her face, and called back to Counselor Abagail. "Yes!" Her voice echoed against the stark walls and floor. "Yes I'm just going back to my quarters first."

Counselor Abagail paused at the door. She didn't understand the reasons behind Caterina's need to visit her quarters at dinner. It had been a pattern at this point, but low on the priority list.

"Counselor!"

She looked up and saw Miranda approaching, almost running towards her.

Her face was shifted and her eyes were wide open. "Come to medical, right away!"

In the dining hall, Elder Cane dropped his fork as several officers came and tapped him on the shoulder. "Pardon us, dear Elder, but we require your presence in medical."

Cane wiped his mouth with his napkin and looked up. He saw Counselor Abagail standing across the dining hall in front of the door. He made eye contact with her as she nodded. Cane got up and dashed over to her.

"What is happening? Has he expired?"

She shook her head. "No sir. But you must come to medical at once. He is awake and lucid."

Cane opened the door to the dining hall and stormed down the hallway as Counselor Abagail followed. He looked at her directly. "What is going on? He's awake and lucid?!"

"That's what Miranda said." She followed him.

Cane's eyes widened. "Then let's go!" Cane started running down the hallway as he called back to her. "Gather everyone! Jeremiah, Eli, everyone! We need everyone there. I'll meet you over there!"

Counselor Abagail ran back into the dining hall and immediately made eye contact with Jeremiah. He stopped eating and lay his napkin down gently on the table without breaking their eye contact. She nodded and he came over to meet her. "The scout is awake," she said, as Jeremiah's mouth fell open. "Shit!" He started out the door.

"Get Eli." she said. "He is at the other end of the tunnel. Where we found him. On duty. He's been watching out since we took the scout to medical."

Jeremiah nodded and flew into the south corridor.

As he ran, his sneakers squeaked against the polished concrete floor. Usually when he walked the south corridor, he went at a much slower pace, and would watch the horizon through the small, rectangular windows that lined the exterior wall, but today he was steady, determined and facing forward. He could see the desolate terrain, in a dismal blue, pale moonlight, from the corner of his eye, as he ran towards the outer portal.

"Eli!" he called as he reached Bay 2. Eli was standing in front of the long, rectangle viewfinder window, facing outside. When Jeremiah called his name, he turned around to face the man.

"Come quick! He's awake!"

Eli's mouth dropped open and his eyes widened. "He woke up? That fast?" Jeremiah reached out and grabbed Eli's arm as the two took the opposite hallway down towards Medical.

When the two men approached the Medical exam area, they stopped at the double, stainless-steel doors, as Jeremiah placed a flat palm against the door.

He turned to look at Eli, who looked up and into his eyes directly.

Jeremiah shook his head. "Cane will probably want to run the show."

Eli nodded and looked down as Jeremiah pushed the doors open, and they walked in to the striking scent of alcohol and disinfectant.

Several overhead lamps were aimed towards the chair that Jeremiah could never forget.

They went to the opposite far wall, which was lined with supply cabinets, and Jeremiah opened some cabinets. After he opened the third cabinet door, he fished a box and flopped it on the counter.

He pulled out two yellow gowns, and handed one to Eli. "Let me find some surgical masks."

As Eli started to rip open the plastic that covered his gown, he looked up at Jeremiah. "What do you think he's going to say to us?"

Jeremiah stopped rummaging through the drawers and looked over at Eli. "Who? Cane?"

"The scout," he said, as he tied off his gown behind his back. "Like…why he is here. Why he came. Do you think he has a message to deliver to us?"

Jeremiah shook his head and continued looking through the drawers. "I don't know, Eli. That's the mystery of the hour. None of us know why he came here."

A familiar gravelly voice called to them, from the opposite end of the exam room, near ME 2. "I have masks over here! Get over here!"

Cane.

None other.

Jeremiah looked over and saw the man shaking his head, standing and looking towards their direction, with his hands on his hips. "Today, boys. We have been waiting for you." Jeremiah and Eli walked briskly towards the door to ME 2 and looked over at Cane.

Cane stopped Jeremiah as they approached the door. "Do you have your questions?"

Jeremiah looked at Cane and nodded.

"Then I want to make sure that you do. You have them written down? Give me the list, and I will hand it back to you when you are speaking with him."

Jeremiah grabbed Cane and they retreated a few feet down the hallway as Eli looked on bewildered.

Jeremiah waited, as he looked at Cane. Cane had wide eyes, and looked back at Jeremiah with fear, and trepidation.

And Jeremiah thought of the condo in Philadelphia. He remembered when Cane lived there, even if Cane did not. Or claimed not to. He remembered a much younger Cane in the lobby of an upscale apartment building just a single block from the river. And Cane had waited for Jeremiah in particular.

"I understand you are coming here," Cane said as Jeremiah approached.

"Maybe," he said. "Jersey's gone. We're all being assigned to living quarters. I got this address and 7B."

Cane nodded. "That's my place."

How did they not recognize each other in the colony arrival yards? Jeremiah didn't bother with an answer. For many years had passed. But Jeremiah had known exactly who Cane was. Even if Cane didn't recognize Jeremiah as a middle aged man. For when Cane and Jeremiah had first met, outside of 7B, Jeremiah had been a child, a teenager, an abandoned orphan at the time.

Jeremiah had looked up expectantly, with big, blue youthful eyes. "So I will be welcome there? With you?"

Cane nodded. "Yes. You will be welcome." And then he looked around, but noticed that Jeremiah appeared to be traveling alone. Cane looked over at Jeremiah. "Do you have any family? Mother, father?"

Jeremiah's eyes fell.

In medical, near ME1, and the room with the scout, Cane placed his arm gently on Jeremiah's, and looked in his eyes, and both men paused, and made eye contact.

The three men paused at the door to ME 2. Counselor Abagail stood at the other side of the room, her head hung low, and rubbing her chin.

The other nurses, along with Miranda and Counselor Abagail's assistant Caterina — chatted next to the plastic bubble.

Counselor Abagail looked up with tired eyes. She pointed over to the bubble, as the three men looked over at the scout.

There was an element of mystery; it was like looking through a layer of waxed paper.

But the dark image, the dark-continent among strange waters, on the small plastic globe, indicated that the visitor was sitting up.

And then there was a moment when the room was silent, until they heard a cough coming from inside the bubble; not so much of a hacking but more like clearing of phlegm from inside the throat.

The scout was a rather uninteresting looking man.

His dark hair – a dark brown, but almost could be mistaken for black – was combed over across his forehead and parted on the side. Stubble grew on his chin, neck and cheeks. Jeremiah estimated a few days' worth. But the man looked, perhaps, like any other man would passing another in the hallway. His skin was now healing, and the man sat up in bed; his eyes were bright and fully open, and he smiled.

Cane stepped forward and looked through the containment bubble. "You've arrived at Sector B Colony. I am Desmond Cane. I am first in command. To my right is Counselor Abagail Winters, my second in command." She nodded at the scout, he gave her a nod in return and smiled.

"Jeremiah Walter is to my left. He's an expert in meteorology and botany. Among other specialties."

Jeremiah shifted his eyes over towards Cane's direction but said nothing. The room was silent as the team looked at the scout, who simply sat in his bed and returned their stare. Cane shifted on his feet as it looked as if the man were preparing to speak.

They gathered closed to the bedside.

The man raised his arm and pointed his finger at Eli, who stood off towards the window. "I have a question for him over there…"

Everyone turned and all eyes were on Eli. He shrugged his shoulders, but joined the group at the bedside. Cane put his arm around the small Hispanic man. "Eli here oversees our security. He spends hours looking for pirates. He was the one who first spotted you."

"As he should have been," the man said softly and smiled. He looked directly at Eli. "Do you remember me, son?"

Cane's eyes widened. He looked at the scout and then over at Eli. "Eli you know this man?"

Eli shifted on his feet and fidgeted. "I…"

Cane dropped his arm from Eli's shoulder and looked at him, over at the scout, who sat smiling and watching them, and back at Eli. Eli looked at the scout and the scout nodded.

"My name is Nelson Moses," the man said. "I have come here with a message for you and your colony."

There was a pause. A brief moment of silence as each of the colonists exchanged glances.

Counselor Abagail finally spoke. "Welcome Mr. Moses," she said. "As Cane mentioned, I am second in command of Sector B. What is this message that you are bringing to us? And who sent you?"

Nelson smiled. "I come of my own free will."

"Then how are we supposed to believe what you say?" She shook her head.

Cane raised his hand. "Just…tell us what you came here to say. I'm not as concerned so much with why you came at the moment. Tell us your message."

Nelson nodded as all eyes turned to him. When he began speaking, his voice was muffled, speaking through the containment bubble.

But his message was clear.

And when he stopped speaking, Cane, Jeremiah, Counselor Abagail and Eli all stood and looked at each other, with wide eyes, and mouths aghast.

After they had finished with the scout, Cane had called another town hall. Jeremiah walked into the auditorium. It was the same amphitheater that they held the town hall in discussing the possibility of traveling to the habitable zone. It had the same rows of chairs which soared downwards to a presentation area below.

It was usually reserved for Cane's town halls, and rarely used otherwise, and today, the town hall was the most heavily attended that he could remember.

He stood in front of a long, wooden conference table set in the middle of the presentation floor, and watched as the colonists took their seats.

The room felt heavy.

As he looked at the colonists in the rows of chairs that led downwards towards the podium and screen, he recalled his days at Drexel.

Back when he had lived in Philadelphia.

As he took a few steps into the room, he looked around the room and waited.

And the chatter died down.

Everyone became silent, and they focused their attention to the front of the room. There was a giant screen installed in the front of the room, which projected an image of the scout for all to see. All that could be heard were the beeps and sound audible of the monitoring equipment, and little else. Jeremiah stood next to Cane, who said nothing. Jeremiah thought, for a moment, of the star.

Didn't he say it was a wandering star?

There was a term for it that he thought they had discussed. Or guiding star. Something like that. He couldn't quite put a finger on it.

And then he slapped his forehead.

What the heck was he thinking about? Had that even been for real? And then he thought back when the star took him on a journey through space.

Jupiter is the answer…

Jeremiah was brought back into the present as Cane took the podium in front of the screen. The colonists waited.

Cane cleared his throat.

When he started speaking, he addressed the group in a solemn manner.

There was a touch of sadness in his voice. "Ladies and gentlemen, welcome. Thank you for coming. I have called this emergency town hall session because of two reasons. One, we have had a lot of rumor and discussion lately of a 'habitable zone', which we had addressed in the earlier session. Also, there is a significant message that we received yesterday from the scout that some of you may be aware of."

There was some chatter amongst the colonists. Cane raised his hands as they slowly quieted.

"As some of you may know, he was an unexpected visitor. Some of you who attended the colony dinner a few days ago where we discussed his arrival are already aware of his presence. Many of you today, especially from the lower ground sectors, are just learning of this news now."

Cane walked away from the podium and back and forth across the floor as he spoke, making eye contact with colonists who sat and listened, who looked up at him with wide eyes. Some bit their lips. Others quietly cried and hung their heads low.

"As you know, this scout has recently arrived, and up to just a few days ago, he had been in – what we believe – was a coma. Not sure if it was a coma as *we* know it, but his vitals were always stable. Anyway, we spoke with him last night and he gave us a message which we are all still shaking our heads about."

Cane turned towards Jeremiah who had been sitting with the others on the high council. "Do you want to start with the questions about the zone?"

Jeremiah nodded and stood. He looked out upon the sea of faces staring back at him.

They were the mothers, daughters, fathers and sons who had come to rely on him over the time they had spent together for protection and guidance.

"As you all know, and I have heard the chatter in the hallways and at meal tables, that there is the rumor of the 'habitable zone'.

We discussed it briefly the other day, and now we have more information on it."

Jeremiah stood and watched the colonists, who were silent and motionless, but all eyes were trained on Cane. He continued as he walked back and forth in front of the conference table. "We need to consider what exactly has happened to our planet to explore the possible existence of this zone. Many of us witnessed the wave first hand. Especially those who lived on the East Coast of the United States of America. And those of you who are younger – who only know life in Sector B, have listened to the accounts of the older population of the colony recount their story of survival and evacuation."

Jeremiah changed the image on the screen which hung high on the wall above the conference table and presentation area to a map, with a giant land mass surround by two massive bodies of water. Several of the members of the high council, who had been seated at the conference table, craned their necks upwards to view the map.

"This is an approximation of what our planet looks like today," Jeremiah said as the lights in the amphitheater dimmed automatically. He turned around to face the darkness towards the seating area as a man called out. "That is Earth?!"

An unidentified female voice also called out from the darkness in the audience. "Are you sure?!"

There were some audible gasps.

The planet looked nothing like anyone had previously remembered. And such a large-scale, cataclysmic event – such a profound seismic shift – seemed incomprehensible. As the graphic rotated and projected in 3-D above the colonists to show everyone the new topography, Jeremiah shuddered at the sight: a massive supercontinent which spanned the entire equator, surround by two massive oceans: one at the North Pole, the other at the South Pole.

After a few minutes of silence, Jeremiah sighed. "That is what we believe Earth looks like today," he said, looking back between the colonists and those on the high council. "This is based on our research and investigation, and we spent several hours tweaking this graphic after speaking with the scout earlier."

A man in the front row raised his hand and Jeremiah nodded. "How can we be certain? We haven't mapped out anything. Do we even have the technology to do so anymore?"

"This is a hypothesis, of course," Jeremiah said. And then he walked over to the podium. "What we *believe* happened – and we are basing a lot of this theory on what the scout said – was that the rotation of our planet slowed, over the course of many decades, which caused a shift in the oceans. The water started flowing towards the North and South poles."

The man in the front row continued. "Still that doesn't explain the wave. How could a giant tsunami flood half the planet so suddenly?"

Jeremiah looked down, and then over at Cane.

Cane's face fell, and looked at the colonists directly. "I'm not going to sugar coat it. But our planet has almost reached a point of its death."

A chatter moved about the room as Cane held his hands up. "Please. Please. Let us finish telling you what the message is."

The man in the front row then stood and continued as the lights raised, bathing the room in stark brightness. "I was under the impression that coming to Sector B was a temporary thing. Granted, it's been years, but my family has always hoped that, one day, the waters would recede and we would be able to return and rebuild. What do you mean our planet is near death?"

Cane raised his hands again. "Please sit down. And everyone, quiet please! Everything will be explained." Jeremiah walked over to the man in the front row. "I'm afraid this planetary shift is permanent." He moved away from the podium and took a seat with the others at the conference table.

"We need to consider what this man has told us," Cane said, quietly, standing and looking around the room, at everyone. Jeremiah signaled his right hand up towards the screen and an image of the scout, in his containment bubble, lying in the bed in ME1. He had fallen asleep in his tent, and the hum of the machines dominated the silence of the room. "This is not something from science fiction movies. If he is correct, we don't have much time."

A woman on the far side of the room stood. "What are the specifics of the scout's message? You haven't reviewed them yet."

Cane nodded. "Yes. Yes. I was getting to that. Please sit." The woman returned to her seat as Cane looked around the room. Jeremiah focused on Cane for a moment, and then, as

Cane spoke, he watched the man's lips move, but Jeremiah only heard water flowing in his mind. There was not a day when he didn't think about the wave.

It was the day when all was lost.

And he was jogged back to the present as chatter waved through the room, flowing back from the front of the room, where the high council sat around the expansive conference table. And the chairs, which had been arranged in a town hall, theatre style, facing the table downwards, were filled with colonists.

Jeremiah stood and addressed the colonists. "The scout spoke of something called a 'wandering star'." Cane snapped his head and gave Jeremiah a dirty look.

Jeremiah ignored it.

"A 'wandering star' is a celestial phenomenon where a collapsed star travels through space –"

Cane shook his head. "– No, everyone, the mission we are forming is to look for the habitable zone. Now is not the time for celestial *hocus pocus*. Yes, our planet is dying. And we may need to look beyond the surface to extend our existence…but our mission – presently – is clear. We need supplies. And we need to find a more hospitable area of the planet to call home."

There had been such an immense interest in what the scout had to say, that there had been a line outside the door before the meeting started – colonists had lined up and gathered around the open door, and spilled into the hallway.

Counselor Abagail sat next to Cane, looking over at him in earnest. She pursed her lips together. Winston was on the other side of the table, and he looked down at his notepad. And then, when Cane looked out at the crowd, where the lights had been dimmed, he made eye contact with Jeremiah, who sat in the front row. Cane stood, and scanned the room, and Eli was also seated in the front row.

A chorus of chatter erupted in the room as Cane finished. He looked over at Counselor Abagail and then over at Jeremiah, who sat back in his seat as others around him talked amongst one another. Jeremiah leaned back, raised his eyebrows and looked directly at Cane.

Cane raised his hands. "Everyone, quiet, please. The side conversations will not help any of you understand the situation more thoroughly."

A man three rows from the front stood and looked directly at Cane. "What did he say? Are we going to find the habitable zone that everyone is talking about?"

Cane raised his arms. "Please. Please, everyone. We have not been able to confirm or deny this purported area. It may exist. It may not. What the scout told us directly is classified."

The man's face shifted and he waved his hands and sat down. "Classified?! Doesn't it affect us all? Why won't you give us a straight answer?"

Cane sighed and looked over at Jeremiah, who shrugged his shoulders and stood. He turned to face the group as Cane slowly sat down.

"Everyone, you have to place your trust in us as your leaders. We have met, and we have decided to arrange a mission to locate this zone and we will report back to you. But until then, you must remain cooperative – "

" – there will be no mutiny. Or any uprisings."
Cane stood as Jeremiah glared at him. "You are
expected to remain in the same order as you
have for the past several years. We will go on
the mission, and when we come back, we will
have more answers for you."

Jeremiah sat and shook his head.

The amphitheater cleared out quickly as the
high council packed up their items and started
to stand. Cane addressed the others. "To the
conference room. Now." Cane looked over at
Jeremiah, who raised his eyebrows.

They filed into a solitary door to the side of the
screen in the presentation area, and they
flopped into chairs surrounding another
conference table, in a small, dark room. Eli,
Winston, Counselor Abagail, and Jeremiah all
looked at Cane who took the head seat and sat,
crossed his arms, and looked back at his closest
leaders of the colony.

After several minutes of silence, Jeremiah spoke first. "You left out the biggest part."

Cane nodded. "Yes."

"And now…they believe that we are on a mission to a zone that may not even exist?"

"Yes."

"And what results are we going to obtain?"

Cane raised his eyes and looked at Jeremiah directly. "Careful, son."

Jeremiah scoffed and leaned back in his chair, waving his hands in the air. Cane turned his attention to the others.

"What about you all? Do you feel that we should have made the announcement to the colony?"

Counselor Abagail looked down at her hands as she fidgeted, and Eli made eye contact with Jeremiah, and said nothing, but it was Winston who spoke. He leaned forward. "I think…at this point in the juncture…that we cannot tell the colonists – anything – about the other details of the message. Because we don't *know* if it even holds any validity." Jeremiah looked up and over at Winston. "So what do *you* think then?"

Winston shook his head. "It's hard to know what to think, Jere. Since he says a neutron star is headed our way – and I don't know what to think about that. I don't even know how to process it at this point."

Cane looked over at Jeremiah. "Do you *know* what a neutron star is, Jere?"

Jeremiah looked at Cane, who sat with his arms crossed, head bent downwards, but eyes looking directly back at Jeremiah. His eyebrows were raised as if waiting for an answer. Jeremiah shrugged.

"I didn't think so," Cane said, and got up. He looked back down at the others. "The neutron star will destroy the planet. It's a failing star – and has probably been on course towards Earth for thousands of years."

"Do you think it had anything to do with the shift? The wave?" Counselor Abagail asked.

Cane shook his head and looked at Jeremiah who shrugged. Cane looked over at Counselor Abagail. "We know so little about what really caused the planet to come to a halt that we can only speculate."

"And do you think science will get us out of this?" Counselor Abagail asked.

Cane paused, placed his palms down on the conference table, and leaned forward. He looked down, shook his head, closed his eyes for moment, and then looked back up at his closest followers. "We don't know if there's any validity to this message. But we can't just sit here and pretend we aren't receiving it. In this case," he said, "we must proceed entirely on faith."

Jeremiah watched Cane fold his paperwork and gather his materials as the meeting drew to a close.

It was if he had heard the room swell in chatter as colonists had risen from their seats earlier and scattered in different directions, but now, they were in the private conference room, alone, with only the members of the high council, and it was those five colonists alone who knew about the true fate of the planet.

How could Cane keep the other colonists in the dark about this?

Jeremiah sat in his chair at the conference table and looked on and watched everyone, but Cane paid Jeremiah no mind. He disappeared through a door on the opposite wall along with several of the other Elders.

Before he knew it, Jeremiah was in the conference room alone. He stood and scanned the room, and headed into the amphitheater.

He was now alone.

The colonists had cleared.

Chairs were scattered in a haphazard manner, just as they had always been after the colony meetings. There were several used cups, some white wadded paper napkins, and a few pens.

He stopped walking just short of the aisle, and turned around and looked at the front of the room.

He shielded his eyes from a brilliant, white flash of light. He placed his hands on the side of his head. "*Aaaa!*"

After a minute or two, he was able to open his eyes again, and looked forward at the conference table. The projection screen was still drawn down half-way, and the same scattered papers littered the conference table. The lights were still on.

And then the flash returned and instinctively he grasped his head and fell to his knees, his eyes shut as tight as they could. But he still saw the light, and it penetrated his mind.

You have not listened to me, Jeremiah.

He felt the reality of his surroundings fade away; no longer did he feel the warmth of the small conference room or the cool air of the amphitheater.

He recognized the swirling, white hot sphere.

There had been a time, years ago, when he saw that sphere. He could remember. He grasped at his throat. And he felt the sear of the headache increase. "You are back! And you come to me again!"

The sphere levitated above him in the middle of the amphitheater, as if there were a rip in time and reality; as the star hovered above the chairs, and, as Jeremiah looked beyond, he did not see the rows of seats nor the steps leading upwards towards the doors. It was the soaring of celestial heavens; the tiny, white stars which dotted the night sky.

Jeremiah recognized the star.

And this time, he knew he was awake and conscious. "I have done everything you have told me to!"

But the star did not reply.

Jeremiah looked at it, as the swirling fingers of light spilled into the room, like flames which reached outwards, but did not burn.

You must lead, Jeremiah. I have called you to lead. They will need your wisdom. Your knowledge.

"But I am not the leader. Cane is the leader."

Prepare yourself to lead them, Jeremiah.

He shook his head. "You're coming to me again…"

You must overcome your own self-doubt. You will never be a leader aggressively. Let them come to you…

And then, just as quickly as it had appeared, the star faded, and he was standing in the amphitheater, staring at the chairs. He looked around, over at the conference table, and considered the options that the high council had been presented with.

Earlier, it had been determined that the mission would proceed under two veils: those who would be going on the expedition – Cane, Jeremiah, Winston and Eli – would be accompanied by Miranda for her medical expertise.

Counselor Abagail would remain with the colony as the first in command in the absence of Cane. But the colonists would believe that they were leaving to find a habitable zone; to locate more supplies, more food; additional water.

But the reason behind the mission: to locate a possible zone of exiting the planet? To escape the wrath of the neutron star?

If the message were true, then Earth would be torn apart by the star's astounding gravitational pull.

All life would cease to exist.

But a means to leave the planet? Colonize elsewhere?

Could that be a reality?

Jeremiah walked over to the conference table, still deep in thought. He stared straight ahead, but only saw the visions in his mind: the wave, wiping out cities, then the radiation and killer heat and dry sand.

He sighed.

His voice reverberated against the silence of the room. "We are almost out of food and water. We need a mission to find supplies. And we are supposed to go on an expedition – from which we may never return – to find a portal to leave the planet?"

He looked down and shook his head, and then got up out of his chair, looking around the room, at the empty chairs, each one representing a colonist.

A life.

A beating heart.

Would they die in vain?

Jeremiah looked out at the empty seats, and thought of the star. And then the scout. "It's a tremendous leap of faith."

PART THREE

THE JOURNEY
BENEATH

There are things known and things unknown and in between are the doors.

- JIM MORRISON

J EREMIAH OPENED HIS EYES and felt the crust on his eyelids.

He shivered and pulled the blanket up towards his shoulders, but it did little to keep him warm.

The team awoke to the scream of winds flapping their tents.

The temperature dipped to astonishing low levels, and the frozen land was a new experience for them – they had been living in the depths of the catacombs, with regulated temperatures, for years.

There was a dark, shadowy object, which some in the team thought was a shipwreck towards the right of the group, off in the distance. When they parked ROVER 1 to explore on foot, Winston ran to catch up with Jeremiah, who was steadfast and determined. Jeremiah was leading as the point, facing towards the north, shifting his view from the ground. He looked down and watched his feet; how the heavy, brown boots dug into the sand, where water once had been reported to be, lapping at the eastern seaboard of the continent. But that was so many years ago.

"Jeremiah!"

He recognized Winston's deep, commanding voice. He looked over at the man, who looked at him with wide eyes. He tugged on Jeremiah's arm and pointed out towards the right. They stopped walking; the sound of their boots cutting into gravel and sand sounded out against the silence of the night. "What is that over there? Eli is asking me, and I can't explain. Do you have any ideas?"

It was an impending, shadowy figure in the distance. The darkness of the silhouette against the pale moonlight looked like it could be a mountain range; its jutting ridges reached upwards, towards the sky, and the even lines were pronounced and sharp, surrounded by a sea of glistening stars.

"Is that a mountain?" Miranda asked.

Jeremiah and Winston stood and watched the shadow. "No mountains out here," Winston said. "Flat coastal plain. We should be off the Carolinas. That's no mountain. And no trenches that I know of."

Jeremiah scoffed. "Where are we? Still along the coast, right?"

Winston held an old paper map in front of him.

"So we are looking at an ancient map of the United States. We're off the coast of…what…North Carolina now? I can't even tell."

Winston stopped and hoisted his backpack across his shoulder, and tossed it to the ground. "Quite possibly."

The others stopped.

"It's freezing," Eli said, looking up and around at the twinkling sky. "Can we stop? Build a fire? Set up camp? Get something to eat?"

Jeremiah nodded, looking down at Winston. He waved his arm at Eli. "Yes, yes. Just give me a minute. Go in the transport vehicle and warm up for now. I want to see what this could be."

Cane stepped forward. "It does not matter. It's at least several miles away. To the east. Heading further east…"

"What's further east?"

And then Cane stopped walking. He looked out towards the object, fingering into the sky, reaching towards the stars. "I know what that is," he said. "That's a shipwreck."

Winston stopped and stared at it. "Are you sure, Desmond? It looks like it's moving."

Cane pushed Eli and Jeremiah aside and joined Winston. "Moving?! What are you talking about?"

Jeremiah and Winston turned and looked at Cane, who was standing still, looking out towards the dark object, the pale moon bathing his face in blue.

Cane broke his trance and sighed. "There is no way that these shipwrecks would have gone unnoticed for this long. Simply no way. And surviving for so many years? Nope."

He turned to Winston, and his face shifted. "It was...how long has it been since the ocean moved to the North? And when the wave came?" He stood and looked at Winston, whose eyes fell.

Winston shook his head, and then looked up at Cane. "I can't remember anymore. All I know is that, initially, the water seemed to recede a little more each day. And the news was talking about the earth's rotation slowing. It's so long ago now. And I'd been so young."

Cane gave Winston a knowing glance and a nod.

Miranda tapped Cane on his shoulder. He snapped his head around. "Elder Cane. My apologies. But I think we should find a place to set up camp."

His face shifted. "Why, Miranda?"

She looked down. "Because I agree with Winston. I don't think that's a shipwreck or a mountain."

"And so how would setting up camp help us? We'd be sitting ducks!"

She looked at him directly. "If we set up camp we won't be tempted to go closer towards it. At least not tonight. And if it isn't what we *hope* it is, the night could end poorly."

Cane leaned towards her. "And how would tomorrow be any different? It'll be dark then too."

"At least then we'll be rested. And able to make decisions with better judgement."

Cane sighed and looked over towards Jeremiah. "How long are we into darkness?"

Jeremiah took a breath and looked upwards, then back down at Cane. "I'd say a few weeks. We have about five months, I would say."

Cane nodded. "So time is a factor." And then he turned back towards Miranda. "But I agree with you. It may not be best to explore something when we're exhausted. We will need a watch. We can set up shifts. Every two hours. We'll have to keep an eye on that."

Eli looked down at the sand. "How are we going to build a fire?"

He was right. They were standing on what appeared to be the coastal plain, and there was no wood and not a tree in sight. "We have to build a fire somehow," Eli said. "We have to eat." He flopped his backpack down in the sand and shook his head, looking up and around. "We need to build a fire, guys. We need to find some wood."

Winston and Jeremiah looked at each other as Cane looked onwards at the mysterious dark formation. "Are you sure that's not a shipwreck?"

Jeremiah and Winston joined Cane, and all peered at the mysterious dark object.

"We can't risk it Cane," Jeremiah said. "Miranda is right. We need our rest."

Cane scoffed. "And we need to build a fire. And there could be a full harvest of wood over there."

Jeremiah turned and looked. He squinted, trying to focus on it. Attempting to decipher what it could be.

"I'd say that's twenty miles away," Winston said.

But Jeremiah wasn't listening. He was watching the shadow. And then upwards, he saw a brightness to the sky that he hadn't seen before. "I think…"

And then it was the star.

I have called on you to be a leader.

He stopped and exhaled, turning around. "This is the best place to stop, everyone. We can set up camp here. We're exhausted and need our rest."

Cane looked up and over at Jeremiah, but said nothing.

"Two hour shifts, like Cane said," Jeremiah said, and then looked at Eli. Grab some extra shirts. One from everyone. That'll at least get somewhat of a fire going."

The group set up camp with the strange, mysterious dark formation off on the horizon, and with the fire from the clothes, they were able to heat up some soup to share.

"I'll take first watch," Jeremiah said. "The rest of you go to sleep. Rest."

Cane stood up. "I will take first watch," he said. "You've done enough. Now go to bed."

Jeremiah raised his eyes as he stirred some of his soup in a small, metal cup.

He nodded, but said nothing.

Winston woke suddenly to a shuffling noise.

He opened his eyes and saw the outline of the lighting tripods through the thin, tent walls, and what looked like a silhouette of Cane sitting in the chair he had flopped into earlier, sitting by the fire, looking out towards the horizon, after Jeremiah had retired.

Winston called out in a harsh whisper. "Cane! Do you hear that?" But he looked forward. The silhouette of Cane's head did not move. "Cane? You awake?" Winston looked over at Eli, who was still sleeping in the opposite bunk inside the tent.

Winston swung his legs around to the dusty floor. Had he been asleep? He saw the heaters running at full capacity. He thought that he was awake, reading his book, and watching Cane drink by the fire. Winston stood, searched for some sweatpants, and went over and peered through the tent flap. He only opened the zipper a small amount, just enough so he could crouch down and peer through. He could see

Cane's feet at the base of the chair. "Cane!" he whispered.

No response. No movement.

The shuffling continued – now far off to the left. It sounded like it was further away from camp now.

He paused with his hand on the zipper. Ever so gently, he started to pull it upwards, and the tick-tick-tick reverberated against the stillness of the night. Once he got it high enough, he was able to get his entire head outdoors, and he looked up and over at Cane. His head was leaning back and his mouth was open. The poor bastard probably fell asleep on watch.

"Cane?" he whispered. But there was no response.

He turned towards the left as the shuffling got closer to their tents. Against a starlit sky, one that was painted with blues and deep blacks, and amidst a scattering of tiny, white stars – he saw a silhouette. It looked to be that of a man, walking in a haphazard, drunken manner.

He looked at the other tents. Zipped tight. Why had he been the only one who heard the shuffling?

He went to Cane's chair from behind and shook his shoulder. "Wake up Cane!"

Nothing. The man's mouth was hanging open, head leaning back against the chair, eyes closed. "Cane!"

The shuffling was closer as Winston looked up and saw the silhouette of an approaching man, moonlight shining from behind, preserving the mystery of who he was.

Winston shielded his eyes to block out the moonlight. The man stopped and Winston called out. "Who…are you?"

He moved forward and knelt down.

"Jeremiah! What were you doing out there?" And then, before Jeremiah had a chance to answer he spoke again. "I thought you went to bed hours ago! Something's wrong with Cane. Come over here."

Winston got up, reached for Jeremiah's arm and dragged him closer to Cane's chair. Jeremiah shook Cane and tried to rouse him from the apparently deep slumber, to no avail.

Jeremiah placed his two fingers on Cane's throat, just below the cheekbone. "Go get Miranda," he said. "Wake up her up. Now."

Winston dashed over to Miranda's tent and ripped up the zipper, calling out her name. Jeremiah slapped Cane on the cheek lightly a few times as Miranda appeared, rubbing her eyes. "What's happened?"

Jeremiah shook his head as Winston joined them. "Winston found him."

Miranda ran into the tent and got her medical supplies. After a moment, she returned, and started to examine Cane. She stood. "He's alive," she finally said. "And stable. But there must be a magnetic field here. Something significant."

Both Winston and Jeremiah turned to face her. "What do you mean?"

Miranda turned and then looked down at Cane. "Cane has an artificial heart. I installed it in him several years ago when his heart had given out. Its installment was one of the reasons why Cane insisted I come along on this journey." She looked up at Jeremiah. "It was before you joined us."

Jeremiah nodded.

"The heart is designed to place the body in a coma state when it senses high amounts of magnetism. It prevents heart attack."

Jeremiah's eyes widened. "So he will be okay?"

Miranda nodded. "For the time being," she said. "The coma is designed to protect the body."

"What do we need to do, Miranda?" Winston asked. "Do we need to return to the colony?"

She shook her head. "For how far we've come, no, I don't think that is necessary. Once we have cleared the magnetic field, then he should come out of his coma."

Winston shook his head. "Let's gather our things. We need to get out of here. I'll wake Eli."

The team sprang into action as Jeremiah knelt next to Cane. The man's position had been unchanged; his head, leaning back over the top of the chair, was leaning just off to the side, his mouth still gaping open.

"The star got you, didn't it?"

Jeremiah assisted the others packing up the tents, and when they were all awake and ready to leave, Jeremiah hoisted Cane over his shoulder.

"He'll start coming to once we have cleared the area," Miranda said as they started heading north. "Whatever that dark structure is off to the east might be the cause of all this."

Jeremiah laid Cane down on the gear transporter cart and strapped him in. As they headed away from the mysterious dark formation, Jeremiah looked up towards the sky.

He spoke quietly. "Is this because of you?"

Eli and Winston turned around. "What did you say Jeremiah?"

Jeremiah waved his hand. But as the feet turned into miles, and as they headed further north, he knew that he had to come clean about his interactions with the star. For the fate of the team – and of those back in the colony, and the other colonies around the world – depended upon it.

They stopped after traveling for an additional period of time, and Miranda checked on Cane. She addressed the group. "I think we're out of the magnetic field now. He's no longer in a coma state. He's just resting."

"Let's set up camp," Jeremiah said. "I need to discuss a few things with you all, and hopefully Cane will be roused somewhat. We could all use some rest as well."

Their journey had only just begun.

It was in the early dark days, when the last fingerlings of sun, which shined against the moon, were beyond reaching land. They had faded finally, as the horizon and the night sky permeated in deep blues and black. There was a certain aura of tension amongst the group.

206

They trudged against the sandy landscape, dragging their feet, exploring around the vehicle.

The team was silent in the early hours of the morning.

The darkness remained; the sky was filled with stars through the hours of the morning as the team slowly awakened.

Jeremiah exited his tent and looked upwards towards the sky. He had been the first to rise. He looked back at Cane's tent, and saw the small lamp on inside, where Winston promised to hold vigil until the rest of the crew woke up.

Jeremiah wished he had a cup of coffee.

How he missed when he could wake and brew a cup, at his disposal, from the press of a button, and then, just moments later, he would have a steaming dark brew, rich, flavorful, robust; and he could still taste the hot liquid in his mouth. He could feel it rolling around his tongue; he could still feel the warmth as it treasured down his throat, and he could still feel the buzzed feeling of the caffeine as it entered his bloodstream.

He picked at some grit in his eye and looked out towards the horizon, where the stars met the sand. And then he turned around, went to the tent, and pulled the flap open. "Winston," he whispered. "How's Cane?"

Winston was hovering over Cane's bed, looking down at the man. When Jeremiah spoke, Winston looked up and over at Jeremiah, raising his eyes.

Jeremiah could see the whites of his eyes against the darkness of the early morning, and he knew the news could not have been good, considering the somber look on Winston's face.

"He's running a high fever," Winston said. "He may have some type of infection. Not sure how he may have gotten it. His heart appears stable, however."

Jeremiah sighed and looked down at several red marks along Cane's face.

He reached out to touch Cane's face and hesitated. "How could he have gotten burned in darkness? From magnetism?"

Winston shook his head. "Radiation maybe? But in the darkness...wouldn't have thought that. There's a lot about this hostile environment that we don't understand, Jere."

"Do you think that we could find him some medical supplies? Perhaps in an abandoned hospital? What did Miranda say?"

Winston looked down at the floor and shook his head. "Everything in that parallel is underwater, Jere. Far too near the Northern Coastline. We would have to travel significantly to the South. I'm not so sure Cane has that kind of time."

Jeremiah looked over at Elder Cane. "He's dying?"

The man was lying in bed, motionless, eyes closed, but he could still see the man's chest rise and fall, every few moments. Otherwise, he looked like he could have been a corpse.

The antibiotics would give him a chance of survival – which he was hopeful for. He knew that the city of Philadelphia lay not far from their current location, only a short distance to the north.

"It's just that Philadelphia is completely underwater," Winston said, a few minutes later, as the team rose and met outside the tents to discuss Elder Cane's condition.

"I realize that," Jeremiah said. He looked towards the north. The stars in the sky reached down towards the edge of the horizon, down to a straight, finite dark edge.

Jeremiah fell to his knees and looked out at the horizon, where the stars met the sands, out towards the new, vast sea, towards Philadelphia, New York and Boston, and where they were certain to be headed – to the watery grave of the north.

And he looked up. "What can I do?!" His voice sounded against the silence. "And when can we go?!"

Jeremiah went into Cane's tent, and pulled a chair from the opposite side of the tent and dragged it next to Cane's bed. He sat, looked down at the old man, and watched his chest rise and fall. "So you are strong."

Jeremiah closed his eyes and thought about Cane.

Jeremiah had looked up as Elder Cane waited until everyone cleared the room, and then he went over to the dining table, already cleared, and sat down.

He reached down into his bag and then stopped. He looked at the door at the far end of the room.

And then he closed his eyes. And Jeremiah experienced something he had never before. He looked into his own mind and he saw the thoughts of another.

For it wasn't always Jeremiah, but Cane that had tried to remember the days before the catacombs. And this time, it was most certainly Cane. And Jeremiah saw when the sun had still been shining; when the sunlight had not been deadly. And then it was Cane who laid back on the bench in the middle of the park.

For when Cane leaned back and spread out, he was back to the days when the catacomb did not exist; the sun was, in fact, still shining. And back then, it hadn't been shining for six straight months, nor was it raising temperatures to hundreds of degrees. Days were still 72 to 96 hours, and the temperatures were still tolerable.

But Cane then lived in the South, in the days before he was at NORAD in the Rocky Mountains and his eventual move to Philadelphia due to the thinning air in the higher elevations.

And Cane had learned about the news from the North.

For the news from the North, at that time, had a sense of desperation.

He had heard about the oceans rising. Some dismissed it, at that time, as greenhouse extremity. And he remembered, once while standing on the ever expanding beaches in Miami, listening to the news in his earbud: they had been discussing the evacuation of all cities in the North: New York, Boston, Philadelphia, Buffalo, Detroit, Chicago, Minneapolis, and Seattle to name a few. As he stood on the sugary sands in Miami, when the waters were receding, day by day, he hadn't thought about the peril that was soon to befall the cities of the South. For back then, it was all about the cities of the North.

And he remembered, once the cities in the North had been evacuated, and flooded at least to the point of covering streets, he learned that the cities in the South – Miami in particular – was destined for a future of dry, relentless heat and scarcely breathable, thin air.

And then, the vision changed, and Jeremiah looked around the dining room, and saw the long, wooden tables, reaching their way across from one end of the room to the other. Certainly the other survivors were back in the bowels of the catacombs.

Dinner was over.

But now, as he was sitting and remembering, and Cane's head plunked down onto the table. And Jeremiah stunned awake, his eyes wide. He looked down at Cane, who slept soundly.

Did I just experience your thoughts?

Cane shifted.

And groaned. And, as Jeremiah sat and took vigil at the side of his bed, and watched Cane's every movement, Cane opened his eyes. "There was a time when I thought you would never make it," Cane croaked. He smiled wanly as he looked up at Jeremiah.

Jeremiah nodded and smiled.

Cane winced. "There's something about my body, Jere. I heard Miranda talking about it. But I couldn't say anything. I couldn't speak. My heart – it's finished, Jere. I don't know how much time I have left."

Jeremiah leaned in closer. "Are you sure? Is that what it is? Was it the magnetism? Or do you have an infection?"

Cane nodded. "The heart is what it is. The infection is most likely from my weakened immune system. Like you said back at Sector B, I should never have come. But I had to. You understand, don't you?"

Jeremiah drew a breath in, closed his eyes, and nodded. "Yes, sir, I do."

Cane made a feeble attempt to lean upwards against his pillows. "So what is the answer then? What are you going to do?"

Jeremiah looked at Cane. And Cane looked like he was waiting for only one thing.

An answer.

"I will be the leader. And we will go under. And find it."

Cane smiled and nodded. "Good. Now get to Philadelphia. Get the map that I told you about. It will guide you. Get yourselves out of here."

And Cane fell back asleep.

The team knew it was the next day from their impenetrable internal clocks that had been ingrained in them when the days were proper; when there had been a time of sunlight, and then of darkness, when things were in order.

There was day and there was night.

Now, with the rotation of the earth stopped, at the very least, the chaos of the epitome of time had taken over. No one could discern when it was. Unless they paid close attention to their inborne body clocks, and listened to them.

Jeremiah emerged into the tent, as the others were sleeping. Miranda sat up and rubbed her eyes.

"Cane's not looking good," he said, with a quiver in his voice. "The magnetic field has done too much damage to his heart.

Miranda sighed and sat up in a huddle.

"So we have to go under, if anything for Cane's honor," Eli said. "Let's get the map." He looked forward; no one was questioning him, at least not at that point.

It was a quiet and unproductive day.

Jeremiah and Winston chatted at the waterline about methods of surviving the deep sea pressure to locate the map that Cane had spoken about. But besides that, Eli hung around the tent as Miranda bathed Cane's body.

That night, Jeremiah dreamed of his days in Philadelphia. It was like he had been flying over the city.

The streets looked the same, yet vastly different. Cars were still moving, and navigating the streets, pedestrians were still roaming the sidewalks...but something was vastly...different.

He still recalled the interstate as it spanned the length of the river, and just through the murkiness of the water, he could still see the bridges in the distance – they had the same spires and suspension cables.

When they arose again, he got up and headed to the beach, and saw Winston, by the water's edge, fishing through several crates of deep-sea pressure suits on the beach near a crackling fire. "The pressure gradient is going to be substantial," he said without looking up. "We're talking a deep dive towards the sea floor. These suits haven't been properly tested, so we're going to be taking a risk here."

"Do we have much of a choice?"

Winston raised his eyes and looked over at Jeremiah. "This isn't a suicide mission, Jere. We're talking about exploring under a significant depth of ocean now. We've been walking on the ocean floor for centuries now, but how old do you think these suits are? Nothing has been made since the shift. These are what…decades old? At least?"

Jeremiah looked down at one of the suits. "Maximillian?"

Winston examined the suit and ran his fingers over the patch. He closed his eyes as Jeremiah shrugged his shoulders.

Jeremiah examined the suits. "Didn't they go out of business before the big shift?"

Winston nodded. "Yeah. Let's hope these still work." As Jeremiah returned to the observation deck, he chuckled. "Do you remember how they used to look?"

Winston's face wrinkled, and then he raised his head towards Jeremiah. "How who used to look?"

Jeremiah shook his head and kept looking at the murky, deep blue cityscape. "Not who. *What.* The old pressure suits. From centuries ago. The Atmospheric Diving Suits they were called. ADS's. I remember seeing them in the maritime museums. Do you remember them?" Jeremiah looked over at Winston and raised his eyebrows.

Winston shook his head. "Well they sure look different here. When they changed the material. Now the pressure makes the suit stronger. No need for the big, plastic bubbles."

Jeremiah nodded and leaned down close towards Winston, smiling. "And so there's no reason why they *wouldn't* work, since the pressure is part of their supply force."

Winston looked up at Jeremiah. "It's a leap of faith, right?"

Jeremiah smiled as the warmth of the fire glowed against his skin.

The water lapped at the beach, as the dull roar of the surf offered its pleasant relaxing sounds against the silent night. The moon shined brightly, bathing the beach in a blue glow. Jeremiah lay in the sand, and felt the cold earth against his bare skin.

He placed his arms behind his head, and looked at the sky. The stars, millions of them, shined down on him. The tiny, white orbs in the sky. "Where are you, star?"

Jeremiah took a few moments, and sat back, back under the tent, as he removed his gloves, and closed his eyes. He leaned his head back on the nearby ruck bag, and thought of the last time that he saw Philadelphia.

When he saw the vast lanes of the Interstate that ran along the eastern side of the metropolis; where the giant bridges reached outwards towards the east, across the river, to New Jersey, the state that he had once called home.

But the last time he saw Philadelphia he knew it was the last time he would see it.

The submersibles were operable.

The "pressure bubbles" as they were called – were the latest technology when Maximillian had still been in operation. Before the wave came, Maximillian was the latest. Like NASA for the Deep Sea. But after the *Great Shift*, that company went to the graveyard as a multitude of other companies had as well. At that point, the business of making money and exploration no longer seemed important.

For money became worthless.

And the business of survival took precedence – and "big business" – which once ruled the land, faded away far more quickly than might have been once assumed.

Winston had the knowledge, from years in the Navy, and his brief employment at Maximillian, as well as an engineering degree, to figure out, at least to some degree, how the contraptions worked. And he had them, back at the colony, in storage for years.

"What about the pressure?" Jeremiah asked. "Are you sure these bubbles will hold together?"

Winston looked down at the submersibles and shook his head. They looked like giant, deflated, clear balloons sitting in the sand. "No. No, I don't know for sure that we're going to survive this journey. I don't know if this is even a worthy cause for so much risk. Will we even survive the hours it will take to go down to the bottom and get the map we need? And what is our back up plan if the map is all flooded out and unusable?"

Jeremiah looked over at Winston. "There isn't something we can use to the South? Some GPS mapping station we don't know about? Away from the water?"

Winston nodded as he continued prepping the submersible. "Sure there is. The South is filled with abandoned facilities that should have plenty of data that we need. But we have to consider proximity. And the satellites are gone and GPS no longer works. Where we are – in our remote location – is putting us at a disadvantage. Norfolk is a day away, maybe more, by foot, and that's how we are traveling right now. You know ROVER 1 is parked where the ground is more solid. But if we stay here, use this functioning submersible to the bottom, then we might have a chance. And, we also have to consider the data. We're heading deeper into the unknown."

"It's an entirely different world now."

Winston nodded.

"Now what about Cane? How can we save him?" Jeremiah asked.

Winston looked at Jeremiah. "We can certainly try to save him."

"But first, we need to get the bubbles operational, because without a map, none of us will survive. I can't say how the new ocean formed, but in our present location, Norfolk is too far to explore, and we are closest to Philadelphia, which is completely submerged."

When he looked around, Jeremiah felt he was in the submersible. But he hadn't remembered leaving.

Had his mind drawn a blank?

He looked out the window.

It looked cloudy and blue; dark and without bliss. But there was something mysterious about what was on the other side of the window. For he knew that those areas, the areas that he had once been acquainted with in his past, were now submerged beneath the water.

As the submersible descended, he again looked out the window. "Will we be seeing buildings soon?"

Winston was studying an electrical panel. "We're an hour away."

Jeremiah shook his head and looked back out the window. For something. For any sign that he might see a city in his remembrance.

There it is. I know it's just below us.

But it was just darkness. The black and the blue. And the cloudy, murky saltwater.

Jeremiah leaned his head against the cool sand and closed his eyes. In his mind, he could feel the current shift their submersibles gently back and forth. He opened his eyes as he felt the direction of the submersible shift from downwards to sideways. "Are we still descending?"

And then Jeremiah woke.

He sat up in bed and rubbed the sleep from his eyes. He heard what he thought was screams coming from the beach. He swung his legs out to investigate.

Still shirtless, Jeremiah hugged himself as he stood on the beach and looked on towards the shoreline.

"The water's warm! It's like bath water!" Eli jumped around in the surf like a school boy. His eyes were wide, and he smiled a giant, toothy grin. He looked over at Winston and Jeremiah. "We're out of the hot zone now, right?"

Jeremiah looked up and behind them. "I'm pretty sure. I think the radiation is negligible at these latitudes."

Winston scoffed. "And you have no shirt on. You *must* be confident."

Eli stripped in front of them, and peeled off his radiation suit, tossing it in a pile in the sand. He stood, after a short while, in a bright, white pair of underwear. He ran up to Winston, grabbed his arm, and pulled him into the surf. Winston followed, tearing his shirt off, as they both laughed and enjoyed the warm water.

Jeremiah looked on as Miranda exited the tent, removed her shoes, and joined him. Jeremiah looked over and saw Miranda burying her toes in the sand as they could hear Eli and Winston frolicking and splashing in the water. Jeremiah finally spoke. "Can we leave him in the tent? Will he be okay?"

Miranda looked up at Jeremiah, back at the tent, and then looked in his eyes. "I don't know, Jere. I've been monitoring him pretty constantly since his heart sent him into a coma. What are you thinking about?"

Jeremiah looked out at the ocean, the new ocean which stretched across the North Pole, and to the other side of the planet.

He nodded, and pointed at the sea with his face. "Out there. I think we need some time. Look at them."

Eli and Winston were swimming, playing in the water, doing the backstroke, splashing each other, and riding the waves, running back, and doing it all over again.

"It's been so long since I've been in the water," Miranda said. "How can it be so warm in such a cold world?"

Jeremiah looked out at the sea. "I was just thinking that. There's so much now that's unexplained. Like there's been some intervention."

And there was a silence between then, as they watched Eli and Winston play in the water like children, splashing, forgetting the trials and tribulations of where they were; what their fate had been; and the uncertainties of the future.

"We need to find that map," Jeremiah said. "We need to get down there. Search through. What's left of the city."

Miranda raised her eyes, looking over towards Jeremiah, who was staring out at the sea. "It may have been washed away," she said. "Give them some time. They need to decompress."

Jeremiah looked over at her. "The beacon Moses gave us will track it. And the bubbles that Winston brought will get us down there. We must find it, Miranda. It's not an option."

She paused for a moment, looked up at him, and touched his shoulder. "But we're not going to find it right now." She looked over at Eli and Winston.

Jeremiah looked down at Miranda, and then ran forward towards the foamy surf. He pulled off his pants and underwear, tossed them aside, and ran into the water, as Miranda smiled.

For a few hours, they managed to forget about the harshness of the world around them. They didn't understand why the water had been so warm. Or why the air just didn't seem as cold right then. For the water should have been frozen, and the air should have been biting and frigid. But there were many things that were unable to be explained.

Later that evening, Winston sat in the tent and spread the three submersible bubbles in front of him on the floor. They looked liked deflated balloons. Something that looked like clear plastic. He leaned down and examined each one closely. Each one had keyboards and monitors built into the material. He was about to test each bubble as the tent zipper was raised and the flap opened.

Jeremiah walked in, still wet, toweling himself off. "Any concerns?"

Winston leaned back, sitting on the cot, his eyes still trained on the three bubbles. After a few moments, he shook his head. "I've examined them repeatedly. Back at East Carolina and twice here. I don't see any tears. No breaches of any kind. Was about to run a test."

"So do you think they'll withstand the pressure?"

Winston looked up at Jeremiah and raised his eyebrows. "They've only been tank tested, and, of course, Maximillian went out of business shortly after the shift. So, I'm not really sure. But what choice do we have?"

Jeremiah flopped the towel on the cot on the opposite wall and searched for a pair of underwear. "Well…"

"What?"

"The way I see it, we have a choice. It's very clear."

"And that choice is?"

228

Jeremiah sat on the bed and pulled on a pair of sweatpants, looking over at Winston. "It's actually pretty simple. We take the risk. We assume the pressure bubbles are fully operational. No breaches. And we search for the map with Cane's beacon."

Winston looked down at the floor and nodded as Jeremiah fished for a shirt. Winston looked up. "And the alternative?"

Jeremiah pulled on a t-shirt over his muscular frame and shrugged his shoulders. "The alternative is we go back to Sector B. Perhaps this mission is too dangerous, with too many possibilities of failure. We are assuming that Philadelphia is just underneath the water to the north. But do we know?"

"Of course not."

"Exactly. Our technology was built for a different world, in a different time. This is uncharted territory, my friend."

"So you think we should return? Back to the colony?"

Jeremiah sighed. "I don't really know, Winston. But I do know this. If we choose to return to the colony, it's just a matter of time. It may be months, or years. At least if we die trying to find this map, we die trying. If we go back to the colony, we just die."

Cane woke up and looked around the tent. He saw Jeremiah and Winston talking, and as he propped himself up on his elbows, and craned his neck to the side, he saw the pressure bubbles lying in the center of the floor.

Side by side, by side.

He coughed and Jeremiah snapped his head in Cane's direction.

"Cane?" he got up and rushed to his bedside. He crouched down next to him and looked down at Cane. "Are you alright? Does it feel like your heart operation is returning to normal?"

Cane raised his arm and waved his hand haphazardly. He shook his head and exhaled. "Listen to me," he croaked. "I gave you the beacon. Why do you doubt where we are?"

Jeremiah stammered. "I – "

Cane nodded and coughed. "Yeah, you. Don't you ever listen to me?"

Jeremiah shook his head. "What is it Cane? What am I missing?"

"Just look at the beacon. You're not far from the map."

"How do I decipher it? It's some foreign technology. No one has ever seen this. Even Winston has no idea of its origin."

Jeremiah rushed over to his cot and fished the beacon from his backpack. It was a small, black device. He tapped his finger on the dark screen, and it lit up, displaying several different menu options, but the icons he had never seen before.

Cane attempted to prop himself up on his elbows. "There's an option for 'plan route'," he coughed.

Jeremiah located the option and tapped it. The screen displayed a map. But it looked nothing like any map he had ever seen before. There was a sprawling land mass surrounded by two massive oceans – one on the North side, another on the South side. He snapped his head over towards Cane, who had shifted to his side to watch Jeremiah. "Where did you get this?" he asked. "What type of device is this?"

Cane reached his arm up and waved him back over as Winston shifted his attention from his inspection of the pressure bubbles and joined them at Cane's bedside.

"Prop me back up," Cane said, holding his arms up. Jeremiah took Cane's arms as Winston fished for some pillows, placing them in a makeshift mountain as Jeremiah hoisted Cane up and rested him against the pillows.

Cane reached his arm out. "Give it to me," he said.

Jeremiah placed the small, rectangular box in Cane's hand. He immediately picked it up, held it closer to his face, and studied it for a few minutes. He tapped his finger against the screen a few times, and stopped. He looked up at Jeremiah and Winston. "Look here," he said, turning the device around. Jeremiah focused on the small object, but the screen was bright and colorful.

"It looks like a map of the buildings in Philadelphia," Jeremiah said.

"Because it is," Cane said.

"It will lead you right to it. And I brought you here. Because it's right out there. Right in the buildings of Center City. When the wave came, I don't think it went anywhere. At least from the looks of it."

"What are you saying, Cane?" Winston asked, reaching for the device and examining it for himself. "Where did this come from?"

"What I'm saying is I remember my old damn address," he said, adjusting himself. "And that thing is still in my old condo, somewhere. Look at the damn cross streets."

Jeremiah leaned over closer to Winston and examined the graphic.

He saw Broad, recognized it immediately. And then the blinking icon flashed on the corner.

He looked over at Cane. "So you believe that it's still in your old condo?"

He sighed. "I don't know for certain. But I can't imagine how the map and the tracking device could have been separated."

Jeremiah sighed. "Why didn't you tell us about this years ago? We could have arranged a mission a decade ago."

"Because I didn't think it was anything real until the scout showed up at the colony. I was visited in dreams. At least I thought they were dreams. And at the time, I didn't think anything of them. Now I'm dying. I'm supposed to be taking care of a colony and can hardly take care of myself." Cane tossed the pillows aside, flopped over and buried his face in the mattress.

Jeremiah leaned back and looked at Winston. "Cane, we still look up to you for guidance. You are still our leader. Don't lose sight of that."

He erupted in a fit of coughing. His voice was muffled. "I haven't done anything."

Winston leaned forward, and placed his hand on Cane's back. "Yes…you have. You've provided us with the key for our survival. And yes…we have to search for it under a vast amount of seawater. But there's hope. You've given us hope, Cane. And for that, you will always be a leader."

They awoke to chilling winds.

The tent flaps, no matter how tightly they were zipped up, flapped and woke them several hours before they had to rise.

Jeremiah mumbled and stumbled out of his cot. Winston was lying in his cot, holding a pillow over his head. Eli was in the next cot, and he saw him turn. Most likely away from the noise.

He made his way over to the bags and pulled some coffee packs and a thermos of hot water.

He ripped the pack and tossed it in a small cup, and poured some water over top. It was surprisingly still hot from when Miranda had heated it hours previously.

He stood, sipping his coffee, and scanned the inside of the tent as the flaps caught the bursts of early morning wind outside. It looked as if Winston fell back asleep. That was fine. Let him sleep. Still an hour before they had to rise.

Eli was tossing and turning on the other bunk. Probably awake and listening to the wind.

Miranda was lying in her cot, stone and still.

And on the other side of the tent was Cane. Still in the same position they left him in last night, lying against the pillows that Winston had propped for him.

Jeremiah walked to the other side to get a closer look at Cane.

He took a stool next to the bed, sipped his coffee, and watched Cane. And thought of their conversation last night. And then, to a conversation they had had, years ago: "Will you ever pass the torch to me?" Jeremiah had asked, as they walked down the South Corridor together.

Cane scoffed and stopped walking, looking up at Jeremiah. "You are kidding right?"

Jeremiah's face shifted and he looked back at Cane. "No, why would I be joking with you? I'm always serious with what you are saying."

Cane took a deep breath and shook his head. "Jeremiah, you have so much to learn about leadership before you can take on this colony. You came…what…a few years ago? You have skills. I'll give you that. That's why you've stayed. But leading? A way with the women doesn't make a leader."

In the tent on the northern edge of the new continent, Jeremiah sipped his coffee as the winds burst outside. He looked at Cane, and after a few minutes, he reached out and touched his cheek, drawing his hand up instantly.

At the same time, he heard stirring in the other cots, as it came close to wake up time.

"You talk to Cane yet?" Miranda asked, through a yawn.

Jeremiah sighed. "Yes," he said. "But he's gone."

Miranda stood up. "What?"

Jeremiah wiped his eyes and set his coffee down. He turned his head around but closed his eyes at the same time. "He's gone, Miranda. I was sitting here for a while. When I sat down, I heard him breathing. But he just passed. Maybe a few minutes ago."

"Oh no," she said, as her face fell. She joined him at his bedside. Winston and Eli came as well.

"So it's just us," Eli said. "Should we go back?"

Jeremiah looked down for a minute. And then he shook his head. He sighed. "No," he said. He looked up the others. His eyes were red rimmed. "We go on."

"But we have no leader," Eli said.

Jeremiah stood up as the others looked at him. He wiped his eyes and finished his coffee, setting the cup down on the bed. "You do have a leader. Now let's go and get this map. If there's one thing that Cane wouldn't have wanted, would be for us to sit around moping and wondering what to do next. So I'll step up. Guys, we have a mission to complete."

Miranda watched the others haul the pressure bubbles to the waterline.

They dragged the giant, clear contraptions, carried by two men, and dropped the bubbles in the sand, just where the water met the beach.

Jeremiah started suiting up. "When will we see the sun again, Winston?"

Winston shrugged his shoulders. "It's really hard to tell."

Jeremiah stopped pulling on the suit and looked at Winston. "Just an estimate, please."

Winston looked down at the sand. "I would say a few more days. Maybe a week?"

Jeremiah nodded and looked at the others. He motioned for Eli to pay attention.

"Okay. So when we descend, it will be pitch black. And then, if all goes according to calculation, when we rise to the surface, it will be even closer to daylight. We'll be pressed to get back to Sector B."

Eli was working on getting his bubble spread out on the sand and preparing it for inflation. "Okay. And so this button here controls the lighting? For the descent?"

Winston nodded.

He continued. "And those little green buttons on the side activate the oxygen chamber. It will circulate an atmosphere for up to a full week. And for deep sea breathing, of course, the perfluorocarbon fluid."

Eli scoffed and smiled. "Wow. How did Maximillian go out of business when they had these? They're pretty amazing."

Winston shrugged as he prepared his own bubble, and looked over at Eli. "Well...they were working on these before the great shift, but then, since their offices were destroyed by the wave, the project fell apart. I had these from my years working on the project, and that's how we got into the colony. "

Eli's eyes widened. "You don't say? How did I not know you had these?"

Winston smiled. "I had to pull some strings, Eli. When we first arrived, they didn't want to let us in. But then I told Cane about the pressure bubbles. And he let us right in."

Eli nodded. "Okay...so we're not going to have to worry about any radiation? If the sun comes by the time we surface?"

"I don't think so at this latitude. The radiation, as far as I can tell, is confined to the tropical zones."

"But you don't know."

Jeremiah raised his eyebrows. "No, Eli. He doesn't know."

Jeremiah leaned forward, close to Eli's ear. "Eli. Are you comfortable with this?"

Eli nodded. "Yes, yes I am."

Jeremiah looked directly at Eli whose face seemed awash with worry. Jeremiah looked over at Winston who nodded.

Winston placed his hands on Eli's cheek. "You don't have to go," he said. "You can stay here, you know. Help Miranda with Cane. She's going to need some help preserving his body. We certainly can't dispose of him here."

Eli closed his eyes, nodded, and leaned against Winston's hand. Eli shook his head. "Oh...I just feel..."

Winston opened his eyes and placed both of his hands on either side of Eli's cheeks. Eli opened his eyes and looked into Winston's.

"I have to go," Eli said. "I have to do this. I need to be a part of this."

Winston nodded. "Then come. And know that this mission will be full of unknowns – "

"– but let's start with what we know," Jeremiah said as he walked up to Eli and Winston. They both looked up at him. Winston shifted his face and pulled away from Eli.

Winston returned his attention to his bubble. "What do we know, Jeremiah?"

Jeremiah raised his eyebrows and cocked his head to the side. "Well, for starters, we know that these bubbles have never been pressure tested. We assume they are operational, of course."

"Of course," Winston said.

Jeremiah nodded. "And then – assuming they hold up to the pressure at what we think could be a mile down – there's the map to find. I mean, what's Philadelphia going to look like now after years under seawater?"

Eli perked up. "We just follow the beacon, right?"

Jeremiah and Winston both looked at Eli, and they watched the man spread out and prepare his bubble, never taking his eyes off of them.

Eli paused for a moment, let the uninflated bubble drop to the ground, and crossed his arms. "I think we all know that we'll be going down blind. Now let's stop bickering."

Jeremiah and Winston looked at each other. Winston shrugged. "Truce?"

Jeremiah nodded and the men shook hands. Winston raised his eyes to Jeremiah. "It looks like Eli may be taking over your role, Jere."

Jeremiah tilted his head and looked at Eli. Such a small, simple man. Reserved and careful. But loving and loyal. He could see that when he interacted with Winston.

And then, he wondered how Eli had found the courage to sign up for security lookout at the colony. And Jeremiah thought, he concentrated on those days, when Winston and Eli had first arrived to the colony. And he remembered when Eli had passed him in the hallway, not far from the entry doors, and Jeremiah had stopped him.

"You're a small man," Jeremiah had said, looking down at Eli, who looked back up at him. "How do you expect to protect us if we should be attacked?"

Eli stopped walking and placed his hand on Jeremiah's shoulder. "It's all in courage."

And then Jeremiah opened his eyes, as they stood on the beach, so many years later, now placed together after years of bonding, on a team that was about to descend under a mile of seawater, to explore the remains of

Philadelphia. Eli looked up from his bubble, and held his stare with Jeremiah for a minute.

And then Eli got to his feet.

He came close to Jeremiah, placed his face close to his, and placed his hand on his shoulder. "I have the courage, Jeremiah. I always have. And courage is what it takes."

Once the bubbles were ready for inflation, they left the contraptions on the beach and retired to the tent. Jeremiah looked over at the far end of the tent, and Miranda was seated near Cane's bunk, wrapping his body in silver foil.

THEY ATE AND RESTED for a few hours and then returned to the beach in their pressure suits. They each wore a grey second skin, with communication devices strapped to their left wrists with small keyboards.

Jeremiah pressed the inflation button on the side of the bubble and it expanded to the size of a giant egg, large enough to hold a man inside.

The bubble itself was clear, and the inside shell lined with navigational and propulsion equipment; it was so thin that it melded into the side of the plastic shell.

Winston coached the others on the operation.

"When the fluid fills the bubble, it will submerge you entirely. This was standard technology for the pressure. When you are submerged, we will communicate through the devices strapped to your wrist."

Eli inflated his bubble and looked at Jeremiah. "What's the fluid?"

"It's an oxygen rich breathing fluid," Jeremiah said. "Similar to amniotic fluid. You won't be able to talk, but you'll breathe just fine. That's what the keyboard on your wrist is for."

Eli looked down at his wrist, and examined the device.

There was a small viewfinder, and several giant blue keys. He shook his head and shifted his face.

Winston joined him and placed his arm on his back. "You can still stay here, if you wish. Don't feel pressured to go. You don't need to prove anything."

Eli paused and looked up at Winston. Eli shook his head. "No. I'm going."

Jeremiah joined them. "You have the key sequence?"

Eli looked down at the four blue buttons. He tapped the one furthest to the right, then the far left and then the two middle keys.

A light illuminated the inside of his bubble, and it shined brightly, like a star in a dimly lit sky. Along the inner shell, a keyboard appeared, with oversized buttons.

"Now you see?" Winston said. "That keyboard will shine through the fluid. It's reflective, so you will see it in the murky water. Just fine, actually."

Jeremiah whistled. "Maximillian had some pretty sweet technology."

"We were ahead of our time," Winston said.

Miranda approached the three as they were about to enter their bubbles. "Cane is wrapped. He'll preserve. How long do you guys expect to be?"

Winston exhaled, looked over at Jeremiah and Eli, and then finally at Miranda.

She stood across from them with a concerned look on her face. Winston looked out towards the sea. "It will only take a few minutes to reach the surface point, but several hours to descend."

Winston nodded.

"I've worked with these submersibles in the past. This is decades old technology, years ahead of its time. But then the shift happened, and the wave came. And you know, the rest is history. The project never made it to see daylight."

Miranda nodded, looked over at the pressure bubbles, then up at Jeremiah. "When do I contact the colony?"

"You don't," Jeremiah said. "Because we will be returning."

Jeremiah looked back at the beach through the clear plastic shell of his pressure bubble.

It was somewhat bleary, as if looking through a streaked windowpane.

Miranda was standing on the beach, watching them propel forward, through the waves, outwards towards the sea.

The eggs crashed through the surf, and Jeremiah steadied himself with the straps.

"Jere – you keeping an eye on Eli? I'm focused on the beacon."

Winston's voice came through the com panel loud and clear. Jeremiah looked to his right and saw Eli bracing the sides of the shell, but he appeared to be strapped in properly. He focused on Eli. "You okay over there?"

He saw Eli's head snap in the direction of Jeremiah's bubble. He saw Eli raise his hand and give a thumbs up sign.

"Once we're out of the surf it'll smooth out," Winston said.

The sea calmed once they were off shore, and Winston had been correct.

The ride became smooth, and somewhat tranquil.

Jeremiah looked ahead at Winston, whose head was looking downwards. Most likely studying the beacon. And then Jeremiah looked off towards Eli, who appeared more relaxed. Not bracing himself like he was.

"Just a few more minutes, and we should arrive at the descending point," Winston said.

Eli finally chimed in. "And then we have to breathe liquid?"

"Yes," Winston said. "We have to breathe liquid."

Jeremiah closed his eyes and felt the rumble of the surf below the thin layer of the shell, and tried to remember the last time he was in Philadelphia.

And despite the significant amount of time he had spent in the city before the shift, he could scarcely remember the layout of the city. He remembered the largest avenues – Broad and Market – which intersected in the center of what was once called "Center City", and at the intersection was City Hall. He remembered the Victorian feel of the building; it had been renovated many times over the years; and he had gone on a tour at one point. But the steeple, on which Benjamin Franklin stood guard over the city, and the golden clock had been the most memorable parts of the building.

Long before the shift, he remembered, in the days of his youth, walking up Broad Street, and in the evening twilight, he would look up, and look down the street, and the clock would be there, a yellow sphere, hovering above the city.

Like the star.

As the bubbles slowed their progress, he looked up towards the sky. "Where are you, star?"

He sighed. What would Philadelphia look like now?

After decades under a tremendous amount of saltwater?

After shifting currents carrying debris through the water.

Would the buildings even still be standing?

"We are honing into the beacon," Winston said, tearing Jeremiah back to the present. The bubbles slowed and floated in the water, arranged in a circle. Winston was to Jeremiah's left, and Eli to the right. Jeremiah looked over at Winston, who was engrossed in the control panel which was illuminated on the side of his shell. Jeremiah looked back over at Eli who looked back at him and shrugged. After a few minutes, Winston stopped and turned to look at the others.

"Are you guys ready?"

He was holding his hand over the blue buttons on the keyboard.

"I have the combination," he said. "The master. But I want to know if you guys are ready for this. Once it starts, the only way I can stop it is to drain the fluid. And if it drains, we're out of luck. These are the only pods I had."

Jeremiah nodded, looked back at Eli, and then at Winston. Jeremiah examined his keyboard. "Review the keyboard again. How do we communicate?"

Winston moved his bubble closer to the others, so they were each floating in the water, the bubbles in a triangle, nearly touching one another.

He looked through the transparent shell to the others. "Type left – right – right – left – center – left – left." Winston stroked the blue keys in the sequence and his keyboard illuminated. He typed a message as the others looked on.

LOOK AT MY MESSAGE.

"Type in the combination," Winston said. Jeremiah typed in the key combination and his keyboard illuminated, as well as the screen along the side of his shell.

WINSTON: LOOK AT MY MESSAGE.

"You see?" Winston said. "Now you, Eli."

"What was the code again?" Eli asked, looking at the keyboard, his finger hovering above the blue buttons.

"Left – right – right – left – center – left – left," Jeremiah said.

Eli stroked the keys and smiled, looking up at his screen:

WINSTON: LOOK AT MY MESSAGE.

"This is how we will communicate while breathing the liquid," Winston said. "And the liquid will protect us from the pressure. So are you guys ready for this?"

Jeremiah stopped for a moment, and looked at the screen; the letters in Winston's message remained on the screen, and beyond the lighted block, white lettering, he looked afar; outwards, towards the endless sea, the waters of a different kind, of another formation, surrounding a new continent in a different world and a new sky.

He closed his eyes.

And when he closed them, all he could see was the star. The swirling, hot, white sphere, accelerating from the outer recesses of the galaxy, moving towards him beyond the speed of light.

He opened his eyes. "Let's do it." He looked over at Eli. "Are you ready?"

He nodded.

"Go, Winston," Jeremiah said. "Let's go under."

Miranda sat on the beach and watched the bubbles move outwards towards the horizon, and sooner than she thought she would, she lost sight of them against the starlit sky. Winston and Eli had been her friends back at the colony, but she had been closest to Jeremiah.

She remembered when he had first come to medical for his evaluation. And since then, they had dined together, walked the halls together, and formed a lasting bond. She looked, one last time, out towards the horizon. She squinted, in a desperate attempt to see the bubbles, but their movement had been too fast, and they were too far gone. She reluctantly returned to the tent.

She unzipped the flaps and made her way inside, walked over to the side workstation. She fished a small light stick from her backpack and opened her communication station.

She placed her face in her hands for a moment, ran her hands upwards, over her forehead and through her hair, and sighed.

"Diary entry. Date recorded below. Cane is dead. The others are en route to the coordinates for Philadelphia at Spruce and 5th. An area called Society Hill. At least that's what they were talking about before they left. Winston said that's where the beacon signal is coming from. And Society Hill is where Cane's apartment was located."

She leaned back in her chair and closed her eyes as a single tone filled the tent. And then it repeated.

She opened her eyes, looked down at her monitor, and saw Counselor Abagail on the screen, looking at her.

"Miranda!" Counselor Abagail said. "I have been trying you for hours!"

Miranda rubbed her face and sat forward, looking into the monitor. "The signal back to the colony is very weak here. We're a great distance away now."

Counselor Abagail's face shifted. "Do you have an update? People are asking."

Miranda's face fell. "Cane is gone."

Counselor Abagail's mouth dropped. "What happened?"

"We were off the coast of the Carolinas and saw − what we initially thought − was a shipwreck. We wound up setting up camp about twenty or thirty miles from it. Turns out it was something that was putting out a tremendous amount of magnetic energy."

"Magnetic energy? What could be doing that?"

"We had our theories."

"What were they?"

"Jere insists it's a star. Something close in the solar system. Maybe a wandering star."

"How would that happen? Shooting out a magnetic field?"

Miranda shook her head. "I don't know, and neither did we. Jere didn't say much else. But what I do know about wandering stars is when they get close to anything – particularly a planet – everything is devoured. Destroyed. It's sucked into the star."

"So that sounds a little far-fetched then. You keeping Jere in line?"

Miranda scoffed and looked around the tent as the winds picked up outside. The reception on the monitor started to fade.

"…And so Cane's heart – "

"He started having trouble," Miranda said. "He hadn't been the same since then. And when we reached the shoreline, just north of Baltimore, his heart gave out and he passed."

She shook her head. "Wow…Desmond Cane. I can't believe he's gone."

Miranda sat back and sighed. "I can't either. He's wrapped, so should make the trip home."

Counselor Abagail cleared her throat and it looked like she was leaning closer to the camera on her side. "Well, that's why we have been trying to call you."

Miranda perked up and leaned forward herself.

"What are you talking about, Abby?" She leaned back and took a deep breath and exhaled.

"Well, Miranda. Mr. Nelson – the scout – he is much improved physically."

She nodded. "That's good news."

Counselor Abagail nodded and her eyes shifted away. "We've been trying to call you because he left, Miranda."

Her mouth dropped open. "Uh…what are you saying, Abby? He disappeared again?"

She shrugged. "It happened two days ago. He got up out of his bed. Opened the door to ME 1. And just walked out."

Miranda's slammed her palms on the desk. "What do you mean he just left? What is going on with security? What about the quarantine?"

Counselor Abagail held her hands up and closed her eyes for a moment, then reopened them. "Miranda. He insisted that he was going to see you all. Once he was healed, and the test results were returned, and after we removed the containment chamber, he said to us that he was planning on leaving the colony and coming to rendezvous with you and the team."

"So he left? What did he do? Go into Miami and find himself a car? "

Counselor Abagail shook her head. "I don't know, Miranda. He left the colony two days ago *on foot*. I don't know if he acquired a car, or what happened to him after he left."

Miranda closed her eyes and shook her head, hanging her head downwards. "I don't know why you let him leave, Abby."

"He's not a prisoner. I wasn't about to force him to stay."

"But his message, Abby. With what he told us. About the star and everything. Don't you think you should have kept him there? You could have had him sedated."

Counselor Abagail looked down and shook her head. "No. I'm not going to keep prisoners. I called you to let you know that he's on his way to see you. I'm afraid I don't have an ETA. But prepare for his arrival, just in case."

Jeremiah, Winston and Eli all looked at each other, and after a few minutes, Winston nodded. He reached over to the panel and pressed the ignition button, and, within seconds, a thick, warm, green tinted liquid started to fill the chambers. They all looked down, startled at first, at their feet almost instantly covered. And each of them, most likely, felt the same emotion: the twinge of regret; of wishing to change the decision. The thought – from all three of the men – that cast the seed of doubt. Could a man really breathe in liquid?

And they were about to discover the answer.

In moments, the liquid reached their shins. Jeremiah looked up and over at Winston. He was looking down at the swirling liquid at his feet. And then Jeremiah looked over at Eli. He was clutching his chest, looking downwards. And the liquid was rising fast in the bubble.

"Trust it, gentlemen!" Jeremiah said. "We didn't come this far to back out now!"

Winston and Eli both looked up and over at Jeremiah. They locked eyes. Each of the bubbles, sitting in the water, facing towards each other, filling with the liquid. The three men looked into one another's eyes, watching their expressions. The wide eyes. Their mouths aghast. As the viscous green liquid covered their waists, filling and reaching upwards, Eli leaned back against the wall and closed his eyes, as the breathing fluid rose above his face.

Jeremiah noticed how much more effort it took, after being covered by the green breathing fluid, to turn and see Winston and Eli.

WINSTON: BREATHE

Jeremiah and Eli looked at Winston, who paused for a moment, and pressed against the shell of his bubble. Their vision was altered and quite different; similar to looking through something translucent.

Jeremiah looked at his hand. The shimmery reflectiveness of the green fluid made his hand appear somewhat distorted; almost alien-like, but still familiar. He balled his hand into a fist, and then opened and extended his fingers. He drew his hand up towards his face, surprised at the great effort it took to move in the viscous fluid. With slow movement which he could scarcely control, he reached for the keyboard.

JEREMIAH: ELI, YOU OK?

He turned his head to check on Eli, who looked back at the other men. He gave a thumbs up and leaned forward.

ELI: OK. FEELS WEIRD. HARD TO BREATHE.

WINSTON: WILL TAKE MORE EFFORT. JUST RELAX.

Jeremiah looked back over at Eli as they each read their monitors, and he saw Eli nod slowly. Jeremiah reach forward and typed.

JEREMIAH: READY TO GO?

Jeremiah looked at Winston and then over at Eli, and both men nodded. He then looked back at Winston who gave a nod and turned around. He struck a few keys and the bubbles started to hum and rumble slightly, as the water agitated around them, splashing upwards, as they each started to sink down, lower, down into the black abyss.

Miranda turned off the monitor and leaned back in her chair. She stared straight ahead but saw nothing. She thought about running out to the beach – and then stopped. The guys would already be underwater by now, and there was no sense in upsetting them. They would find out about the scout, sooner, rather than later.

Jeremiah looked up, towards the sky, as his bubble started to sink downwards.

He watched the tiny, white stars, and looked over towards the moon, as the water rose across the sides of his pressure bubble. And then, when the water overtook the bubble completely; when the moon was a wobbling white mass, briefly seen through the murky seawater, Jeremiah closed his eyes.

And he saw the swirling hot, white sphere in front of him.

Go, Jeremiah. Seek the truth. Find what you are looking for.

Trust yourself.

Jeremiah opened his eyes, but could see nothing; only the reflection of dark seawater and murky sand floating around the exterior. He could see Winston's and Eli's illuminated bubbles a short ways ahead, and they appeared to be descending at equal speeds. He looked up, towards the crest of the bubble, and they were deep enough that they were covered in seawater, silt and sand; there was no longer a sky of stars, no more a reflective moon. Just water and darkness.

Was this to be their grave?

He reached forward and hesitated.

Look deep within and trust yourself.

JEREMIAH: DESCENDING TOWARDS BEACON?

He saw movement in Winston's bubble but could not see any details in the darkness of the water. Just the lights through the murky distance. Jeremiah looked at his screen and waited. A blinking cursor repeated it's flashing on the left edge of the screen.

WINSTON: CONTINUE DROP. LIGHTS
ON. ELI?

ELI: OK

JEREMIAH: LET'S DO IT.

The three men punched an additional
combination in their blue keypad, and one by
one, the lights on the undercarriage shined
down through the water. Jeremiah looked
downwards, through the translucent floor, and
his mouth dropped open –

JEREMIAH: YOU SEE THAT?

He saw the remains of Philadelphia.

But it was a skeleton. It was not the city that he
had remembered when he was a child. Their
high powered lights scarcely illuminated the
leftover city. No longer were the three
suspension bridges – Walt Whitman, Benjamin
Franklin and Commodore Barry – intact and
perched above the Delaware River to carry
people from the east end (New Jersey) to the
west end (Philadelphia and its suburbs).

He looked down and saw a shell of a city,
submerged in a watery grave and hardly
recognizable.

They were descending right upon it; and despite the darkness of the water, no matter that the city had been inundated under salty seawater and viscous undercurrents for years, the buildings – while a shell of their former selves prior to the wave – were still somewhat recognizable.

They floated by the spires and cables of the Walt Whitman Bridge; the same bridge where Jeremiah had been stuck, sitting in traffic as the coast was evacuated. The bridge had crumbled and fallen; there were gaping holes in multiple places, but it was still intact, though covered in coral and muck.

Closer towards the city, they could see the outlines of cars still parked along the avenues – now covered with silt and sand. A strange, white, sea creature crawled out of the passenger window of one of the cars.

Streetlamps still soared and reached upwards from avenues that no longer heard the hum of traffic; trees still rooted in the ocean floor, long since dead and covered with coral, but they were still recognizable for what they had once been.

They navigated the bubbles through the widest avenue they could find. Jeremiah could still recognize the brownstone walk-ups on Spruce. He could still make out the outline of the stairs; the layers of muck looked as innocent as a fresh fallen snow.

It was like the city had been put on pause. Like it had been frozen in time for years. Like it had just been on the mornings of winter blizzards. And when he looked down Spruce, the street which reached westward in the middle of Center City, it could be easy to deny what had happened.

Until he raised his head.

And saw the shells of the buildings; some of them had buckled under the pressure; brick townhomes caved in. Skyscrapers collapsed to half their original size.

JEREMIAH: CANE'S CONDO?

He looked forward at Winston's bubble.

He could easily recognize Winston's features; the water seemed to be clear at this depth. Less agitated. The layer of muck which covered Spruce, the parked cars and trees, was untouched and undisturbed.

WINSTON: FOLLOW ME.

Jeremiah accelerated his bubble forward, keeping an eye on Winston, and then, just as they were about to turn on Broad street, he noticed that there were only two bubbles.

JEREMIAH: WHERE'S ELI?

Jeremiah slowed his acceleration and watched as Winston rotated and stopped a few feet in front of him.

WINSTON: ELI, COME IN.

No response.

Jeremiah looked up at the dilapidated, crumbled buildings. The light shined on rusted steel beams and broken windows. His eye caught a beam of light; it appeared brilliant and white, as if beaming directly at him, and despite the depth and murkiness of the water, it shined against his eyes, directly towards him. And it seemed...like a star.

And then he thought of the star.

The wandering star.

The one who came to him in his thoughts; when he closed his eyes, when he slept. The star which had guided him through; which gave him motivation and advice. Was that the star? The star that wandered with him? Alongside him? The star which shined above him?

He closed his eyes.

Are you with me? Are you there? Are you there, star?

But he didn't hear an answer.

And when he opened his eyes again, he looked towards the light, and the twinge of hope faded with the light. For the light had been merely a reflected on a broken glass window, the light from his bubble, reflected back towards him.

WINSTON: JERE, GO FIND ELI. I WILL GET THE BEACON.

Jeremiah broke from his musing and looked over at Winston.

JEREMIAH: YOU SURE WE SHOULD
SPLIT UP?

He nodded.

WINSTON: WE MUST SURFACE IN 30
MINUTES.

Jeremiah watched as Winston rounded the corner and disappeared into the skyscraper graveyard. He typed on his keyboard.

JEREMIAH: ELI, YOU THERE?

He waited and scanned the area.

How could they have lost Eli? He raised the bubble up a few feet, so he could see inside one of the buildings, and he paused for a moment. There was a couch in the center of the room he was peering into. A couch. And what looked like the remains of a small table, and some chairs. Still sitting there, untouched, for years.

They hadn't been swept away by any currents, or eaten by any sea life. They were covered in muck and sand, but still recognizable as furniture.

And then Jeremiah caught a glimmer of green light in the corner of his eye. A glowing star, perhaps?

He snapped his head to the right and reached for his keyboard.

JEREMIAH: ELI, STAY PUT. I'M
COMING FOR YOU.

Jeremiah turned his bubble around and accelerated as fast as he could go. He zipped down Spruce, above the cars and trees, getting higher, until he was above the city.

He could see the network of streets and avenues, and looked over towards the suspension bridges that had once linked Philadelphia to New Jersey.

JEREMIAH: ELI STAY PUT. I'M
SEARCHING FOR YOUR LIGHT.

He hovered the bubble over the city and aimed his search light through the streets and avenues; he took a route along the river, inwards towards where City Hall once stood, and then back.

Still no Eli.

JEREMIAH: WINSTON, YOU HAVE THE BEACON? NO ELI YET.

No answer.

He looked at the timer on his monitor. The countdown began when Winston had said they only had 30 minutes left of breathable fluid, in giant red numbers in the corner of the screen.

JEREMIAH: WINSTON? COME IN.

And then a strong current almost toppled his pressure bubble to its side. The wave came through like a force, and once Jeremiah steadied himself, he looked outwards towards the bridges.

A dark, floating object.

Massive; shadowy; moving.

Could it be a whale?

He reached for the instrument panel. The light below repositioned itself and shined ahead. He still could not determine what the giant figure was.

An alarm rang into his earpiece and he looked at his monitor.

BLOOD PRESSURE EXCEEDING SAFE
LEVELS.

He turned his head back towards the bridge; he saw more movement, and braced the edges of the bubble, as another forceful wave toppled the bubble on its side. It floated down to the bottom, and just at the base of the remains of the Walt Whitman Bridge, it rested on its side.

Jeremiah.

He came to.

He was lying flat on his back on the wall of the bubble. How long had he been out? He sat up as quickly as the breathing fluid would allow him to.

He looked over at the bridge.

Whatever the dark figure was appeared to be gone.

The water, however, was not as dark as before. The murkiness had lightened somewhat, and Jeremiah felt that he could see through it to a greater degree.

Had the sun risen?

And would the sunlight even filter down at a depth this great?

And then he felt a feeling of relaxation come over him. It became easier to breathe.

Trust yourself, Jeremiah.

Trust in me…

He closed his eyes.

He didn't feel the need to look ahead, to determine what might be lightening the darkness of the waters, because he already knew. He was still; his eyes remained closed, and he waited.

He listened.

He could hear the bubbling of the waters outside that surrounded the bubble. And then he felt a rumble.

He opened his eyes, and saw the shining sphere in front of him, as the sand and silt rose around the bubble, clouding his vision.

Trust in me, Jeremiah...

He felt the bubble levitate.

The equipment blacked out, and the entire area rumbled as if the earth were quaking. Buildings started to crumble around him as the dilapidated, rusted beams fell to the ground, and clouds of silt and muck surrounded him. But he felt the bubble was moving.

Upwards.

When he looked in the water, the silt clouds were now below him, and the quaking earth was no longer felt.

He was rising, upwards from the death city, higher, faster, and with more force, to a point where he was pinned against the underside of the bubble, and when he shot out of the water, into the air above, he blacked out.

PART FIVE

THE STAR

It is not in the stars to hold our destiny but in ourselves.

- WILLIAM SHAKESPEARE

JEREMIAH AWAKENED and saw stars.

He saw the same familiar stars that he had looked up to, in a night sky, from when he was a child, up until recently. There they were.

Those same familiar stars.

And he noticed something else.

He was breathing air.

Air!

He leaned his head back, laughed for a moment, and breathed in deeply.

Oh, how he had missed air.

It felt so light; so easy to consume. It was tasteless but still managed to taste so good. So delicious!

He felt the cool air soar into his lungs, and he cherished each light and whimsical breath.

He opened his eyes and propped himself up. He had emerged near the beach, just beyond the surf. He recognized their camp just on the edge of the beach. He could smell the smoke of a fire. Had Miranda managed to build a fire?

The moonlight reflected on the water, which seemed unusually calm. He opened the hatch and water poured in. The sting of the cold water shook him awake, and he moved quickly. He looked towards the shore, and when he had caught the surf, he rode a wave to the beach.

"Miranda!"

Silence.

He got up and ran through the sand towards the camp as Miranda emerged, waving her arms. "Jeremiah!" she said. "We thought you were lost!"

Jeremiah leaned against a tent pole and stopped to catch his breath.

Miranda hugged him, but Jeremiah did not return the embrace. She released and stepped back, looking him up and down, her face twisted. "Jere?"

Jeremiah looked down. "We lost Eli. And I lost touch with Winston. I think he's still down there."

Miranda's face softened and she placed her hand on Jeremiah's upper arm. "No," she said. "We thought we lost *you*. Now come let me take you inside! Let's warm you up! I have so much to tell you!"

Jeremiah didn't understand what Miranda was referring to, but he felt a twinge of hope. How long had he been down there? Would he still have any breathable fluid left? Jeremiah closed his eyes and hung his head low.

Miranda grabbed his arm and pulled him towards the tent.

She reached down, unzipped the flaps. Jeremiah grabbed one and held it off to the side as they walked into the tent. Jeremiah felt a reassuring blast of warm air against his face.

But when Miranda stood off to the side and he got a clear view of the interior of the tent, he saw the same cots surrounding the tent walls, the same communication station that they had set on the side wall. But in the center of the tent, at the small table, was Winston.

And Nelson.

"Nelson?! How did the scout get there? Wasn't he back in quarantine?" Jeremiah's eyes widened and he dropped the tent flap and stepped inside. "What – Winston – how did you get inside here? I thought you were still down there?"

Winston smiled and nodded. He stood and walked over to Jeremiah, hugging him.

Jeremiah hugged him back, but his eyes remained wide and questioning, and he stepped back. "Winston?" Jeremiah looked around the tent. "Am I dead? Is my dead body lying down on the streets of Philadelphia?"

Miranda let out a chuckle and reached for Jeremiah to place her arms around his shoulder. "No…no. Jere, we are here and we were waiting on *you*. You somehow got lost. Gone for hours. But you're here! It's a miracle!"

She stood back, held his arms, smiled and looked up into his eyes.

He didn't understand this. It seemed so surreal. "Where's Cane?"

"I wrapped him, and he's preserved and waiting to go back to the colony for burial," Miranda said.

Winston placed his hand on Jeremiah's shoulder. "I wouldn't have left you, you know that right?"

Jeremiah looked at Winston's hand.

There were fresh scars that stood out against his dark skin.

"What happened, Winston?" Jeremiah looked Winston in the eyes. Winston ushered Jeremiah over to the table. The two sat across from each other. Miranda and Nelson took the other two chairs. Jeremiah looked up at Nelson. "I don't even know how you got here," he said.

"What happened to you, Jeremiah? Where have you been for almost twelve hours?" Miranda asked, leaning forward.

Nelson looked directly at Jeremiah, but giving him a knowing stare. "Yes...what happened to you?"

Jeremiah leaned back, sighed, and looked up at Winston. "I thought you were looking for the beacon. That's the last I know. You cornered around Broad, and that was the last I saw of you. I was going to look for Eli." Jeremiah's eyes widened. "Oh! Did you ever find him?"

Winston smiled and nodded. "Yes. He is badly injured, but alive. He is resting on the far cot, and we have him sedated."

Jeremiah looked at Miranda, Winston, and then Nelson, and then back at Winston. "So…what happened to you?"

Winston took a deep breath and leaned forward.

He looked down at the table as he spoke. "I found Eli as soon as I cornered Broad. Just outside Cane's Condominium, actually. He was hurt badly, but conscious."

"What happened to him?"

"He said he saw a massive dark figure that was making strong waves. One of the waves hit his pressure bubble in such a way that it toppled it fast against one of the buildings – and Eli hit the opposite wall – hard. He has some internal injuries."

Jeremiah leaned back and placed his head in his hands. "Oh, no…"

"We hope he will live," Winston said. "As soon as I came across Eli, I linked our bubbles together, and surfaced."

Jeremiah looked up. "So you didn't find the beacon?"

Winston shook his head. "No, I didn't find it."

Nelson leaned forward. "And that's where I come in."

Jeremiah looked perplexed but Miranda smiled.

"What is that?" Jeremiah asked, pointing towards the sky. There was a bright object, which looked like a star. Something cosmic. But most definitely brighter than the other stars.

Jeremiah heard Nelson call out in the middle of the evening silence. "Come on! I have something to show you!" After talking around the table, they headed out to the beach with an old bottle of whiskey. At least a century or two. They had sat on the beach for hours, and all had fallen asleep.

At least Jeremiah thought so.

He looked up at the sky, to where Nelson had been pointing. It was bright, spherical, and appeared to have lighter colored petals reaching out from its core. "What is that star? Is that a planet? Something with gasses shooting out of it?"

And then Jeremiah remembered looking up towards the sky, years before, before the catacombs beneath Miami; before the days when they had left the comfort and safety of the colony, and there was a difference to it.

Speak to me, Jeremiah. You have been called to lead them. Trust yourself.

Jeremiah sat on the sand and listened to the dull roar of the surf. He grasped his arms around his knees, and looked up. "Where are you, star? Why have you abandoned me?"

Nelson sat across from Jeremiah, on the other side of the fire.

"Is that what you believe, Jeremiah? That you are alone?"

Jeremiah looked at Nelson. His eyes were intense, but his face was warm and friendly.

Jeremiah sighed and shook his head. He looked out at the ocean. "I don't know what to believe anymore."

Nelson got up and sat back down next to Jeremiah. They each took another swig of whiskey.

Nelson swallowed and looked up to the sky. "You know, that star up there?"

Jeremiah looked up at the sky as well.

He saw the star in plain sight.

Larger, brighter than the others. And it seemed to have a gaseous tail as well. Like a flower. Moving out in all directions.

"It's a wandering star," Nelson said. "And its presence out there, in that vast place we call outer space, is why I came to see your colony in the first place. And why your friend saw me, years ago, when he was still in High School."

Jeremiah looked up at Nelson. His face had an orange glow from the reflection of the fire. "Who? Eli?"

Nelson nodded.

"So you've known about this all along? The wave, the shift, everything?"

Nelson leaned forward, resting his elbows on his knees. "The shift and the wave weren't really the problem, Jeremiah. Humans can adapt. And you have. It's what's up there – in the sky – that's the true problem."

Jeremiah looked up at the star. It didn't even appear to be moving.

"Do you remember when you interviewed me back in medical?"

Jeremiah nodded.

"What did I say?"

"You said there was a neutron star heading towards the planet. And that there was no other option but to leave."

Nelson leaned back. "But I've come for you. Do you trust me, Jeremiah?" He looked Jeremiah directly in the eyes. "Do you believe that I can save you?"

He looked down and hung his head between his knees, and listened. Watching and waiting. He took a deep breath, opened his eyes, and looked down at the map, which lay in the sand next to him.

"I was always supposed to lead," Jeremiah said. "I would have these visions…telling me to lead."

Nelson looked at Jeremiah and smiled. "We've been watching you for a long time, Jeremiah. Not just you, but everyone here. We're not here to be hostile. We're here to save you."

"How can you save these people? If what is reported to happen is true?"

He paused for a moment and thought of the scout, when he had first arrived. So lost, so helpless. Or so it seemed. All he could remember was leaving him in ME 1 back at the colony. And then he closed his eyes again.

"Jeremiah, you all saved me, didn't you?"

He opened his eyes and looked up.

There he was, Nelson. Now standing before him. His hair caught the wind as he smiled, and knelt down next to Jeremiah. "You have come this far," he said. "You found the map that I gave to Cane decades ago I see."

Jeremiah looked at the scout and his mouth dropped open.

"Wait a minute. You…knew Cane?"

He nodded and looked back at Jeremiah.

His eyes were warm and friendly. "Yes, Jeremiah. I have visited this planet before. Long before you knew your fate, we have known it."

Jeremiah paused and looked at him. The visitor smiled. "Do you understand, Jeremiah? Do you understand what I am telling you?"

He shook his head and looked down at his feet. "This is incomprehensible…"

"…But it's true, Jeremiah. It is what has happened. Would you like me to show you?" The visitor held out his hand. Jeremiah looked at the man's open palm, waiting, patiently, to be held. "Take my hand, Jeremiah."

Jeremiah stood on his feet, dusted himself off, as the visitor made eye contact with him, and again smiled. He raised his eyebrows and craned his neck forward.

Jeremiah looked again at the visitor's hand, still open, waiting. "Do what you believe is right, Jeremiah. Take my hand, if you will."

And Jeremiah reach his own hand out towards Nelson's, and just before their fingertips touched, he hesitated for a moment, and pulled back. Jeremiah took a breath and looked in his eyes. They locked eye contact for a moment, and all they could hear was the crackling of the fire and a light passing breeze.

"You don't have to, if you don't want to, Jeremiah. But what I told you, back in the colony, is true. By taking my hand, I will show you how we got to where we are. And where I am from. You have to trust me."

Jeremiah closed his eyes and placed his hand in the visitor's, and the man closed his fingers around Jeremiah's, and pulled him gently closer to him, and then reached over to take his other hand. Once their hands were clasped, Jeremiah opened his eyes, for a moment, and then there was a brilliant, white flash of light.

Jeremiah shut his eyes so tight that they hurt. "Lean your head on my shoulder, Jeremiah. And listen."

"Now open your eyes, Jeremiah. And hold close to me."

And when he opened his eyes, they were looking down at Earth.

There she was.

The delicate blue marble.

It looked so vastly different now. And he remembered his dream about the star. And what the star had shown him. That massive supercontinent near the equator; it seemed so unreal. They floated in space, levitated together, as Nelson hugged Jeremiah close to him. "Look beyond Earth. You can see the star. Closer. We see it now."

Jeremiah looked beyond Earth, and in the distance, he got a close up view of the star. It was elongated; from top to bottom, the exploding gases fingered from top to bottom, and now, with a commanding view, Jeremiah could see the tail quite clearly. He continued his gaze as he could hear Nelson breathing.

Jeremiah took his eyes from the star for a fleeting moment, looked at Nelson, who was engrossed, staring at the star. "Is it traveling? Moving?"

"Watch, Jeremiah," Nelson said, as he pointed down towards Earth.

Jeremiah gasped.

It was not the Earth they had just seen.

It was the Earth from so many millions of years; he recognized the United States instantly; and all seven continents were surrounded by seas of blue.

"Have you taken me back in time?"

"Watch."

He watched the planet Earth – and as the seven continents that he so clearly recognized were changing; the brown and green land masses shifted, as towards the center of the planet, the land lengthened, as the blue waters retreated from the equator. Before his eyes, he saw the blue reach upwards as the browns replaced them.

He snapped his head towards Nelson, who smiled in return. "Keep watching," he said.

The super-continent formed, slowly, around the center of the planet. The Caribbean dried up, and became a giant land mass. But as it did, Nelson placed his arm around Jeremiah's shoulders. He leaned in close, and whispered into his ear. "This is what was happening, Jeremiah. This is why you have struggled for so many years now. The planet changed. It changed. And it happened. There was nothing that you could do to prevent this."

"How could something like this happen so quickly?"

The visitor released his grip of Jeremiah's hands and placed his arms around him, holding him in a cradle, raising him up in a position so he could still see Earth. "It happened over many years," he said, as Jeremiah studied the new terrain of the planet. "But when the sun started to lose its energy, the Earth's rotation slowed. And when it slowed, that caused the oceans to flood the poles, and retreat from the equator. When the rotation stopped, it caused the environment that you have grown accustomed to living in during recent years."

"They had been talking about a habitable zone. Like we could start over."

The visitor nodded and pointed in the horizon beyond Earth. "Look out there," he said. "Do you see that?"

Jeremiah looked to where he was pointing and squinted. "All I see are stars."

"Look more closely."

Jeremiah studied the panel of space that the visitor was insisting that he examine more closely. He leaned forward, with the mighty Earth just below him, as they levitated past the blue planet and got a closer look.

"There is one brighter star," Jeremiah finally said. "The same one we have seen."

"And *that* is why you must leave with me."

"Why?"

Nelson looked down. "I am not going to show you that vision. This is the point where you must trust me."

Jeremiah took a deep breath and released it. For a moment, he looked at the planet. Which now, with the giant land mass spanning the equator, looked so different than the planet he had discovered as a child. He raised his eyes to look at Nelson. "So...you need me to have faith in you?"

Nelson smiled.

"Yes. It's all about faith. You took a leap of faith when you left the colony. And where did it get you?"

Jeremiah cocked his head to the side. "Well...I..."

"You are still alive, after a test of your abilities. That mission to find the map in Philadelphia would stretch any man to his limits. You breathed *liquid*. You went under a mile of ocean. Look how much you have grown by taking that leap of faith. Look at what you have done."

Jeremiah looked at Earth, and focused on the area of the northern coast of the supercontinent where the camp was sitting.

He saw the massive ocean that reached from the shoreline to the North Pole and back around the opposite side of the planet.

"They're down there," Jeremiah said. "At the camp." Jeremiah leaned forward as Nelson held onto him.

"I think I can even see the formation of the beach where we set up tent," he said.

Nelson scoffed. "You think you can see that from up here?"

Jeremiah laughed. "Well…maybe not."

Nelson turned Jeremiah's head towards the direction of the star. "You see?"

Jeremiah looked at the pallet of beauty before him. For when he raised his eyes from looking at the blue marble, he looked beyond, and saw the approaching star, the white, swirling sphere in the center reached upwards, and down, and the tail was far more pronounced.

"Look to the left, Jeremiah. Don't focus on the star. Do you see it? What I am showing you?"

Jeremiah focused and concentrated hard on the region to the left of the wandering star. He saw something. A sphere. Perhaps a planet? And then he recognized the pastel, swirling colors that rotated around and around.

"Jupiter," Nelson said. "That is the key. I'm only a catalyst. And you can choose to believe me...or not. But here is what I leave you with. Believe. And you will be saved."

Jeremiah woke to a dying fire.

The flames were gone, and so was Nelson.

Jeremiah propped himself up on his elbows, and looked around the beach.

It felt early.

Despite the incessant darkness, he still had some sense of the hour.

The waves crashed just feet away.

He could hear the splashing of the surf. The charcoal smell of the smoke from the fire still permeated the air. And the sand remained cool and damp. He looked around.

Had Nelson gone to bed?"

Jeremiah walked to the opening of the tent. "Nelson, you awake?"

He heard a scuffling in the darkness. After a few moments, Miranda appeared. She was bleary-eyed. "What is it, Jeremiah? Have you been on the beach all night?"

Jeremiah stepped inside the tent. "Where's Nelson?"

Miranda coughed and rubbed her eyes. "Who?"

"Nelson. The scout. Where is he?"

"Where is he? How much whiskey have you had? I think it's time for you to hit the hay. It's still early. We head back in the morning. As far as I know, he's back in ME1."

She padded back over to her cot and flopped onto it. She laid her head on the pillow and closed her eyes. "Get some rest, Jere. We start a long journey in just a few short hours."

Jeremiah couldn't sleep.

He stared at the ceiling of the tent, and watched the seams flap from the strong winds that started shortly after he retired. There was nothing else to say. Had it all been a dream?

It's a leap of faith.

The next morning, Jeremiah was surprised to see Eli up and walking about.

"I hate the darkness," Eli said. "Won't the sun rise already?"

Winston stopped and looked back at him, pulling his t-shirt on. "That's why we're heading back. We want to be back before the sun rises. And we are still days from that I would imagine."

Jeremiah hung his head down and rubbed his eyes.

"Oh hey, Jeremiah," Winston said. "Glad to see you are feeling better."

He looked up at Winston, his eyes still bleary with sleep.

"Feeling better?"

"Oh yes. You were pretty drunk last night. Passed out by the fire."

Jeremiah looked up at Winston. "Where is Nelson? He was here last night. By the fire with me."

Winston's face shifted. "Nelson? Are you sure?"

Jeremiah stood up fast, and Eli looked at him.

"Eli! You're feeling better?"

Eli smiled. "Feeling better, Jere?"

Jeremiah placed his hands on his hips and looked around the room. "Okay, what is going on here, guys? Where's Nelson? I thought he came here from ME1?"

Winston shook his head. "What are you talking about, Jere?"

"The scout! How many fucking times do I have to say it?!"

Winston stood back and held his arms up. "Woah. You need a few minutes?"

Jeremiah took a deep breath. "No. I just need to know what's going on. Where the scout is. Something for this fucking headache."

Winston leaned in closer to Jeremiah. "There is no scout. He's not here. We don't know what you're talking about."

Jeremiah scoffed. "So you are saying that everything that I experienced is a figment of my imagination?"

Winston led Jeremiah and Eli over to the table in the center of the tent as Miranda joined them. They sat and Winston looked Jeremiah directly in the eyes. "I don't know what you are talking about, Jere. This scout. Who is he? Where did he come from?"

Jeremiah sighed. "He came to the colony! ME1. Why don't you remember him? He was just here last night!"

Miranda leaned forward. "Last night we pulled you from the ocean. You were out cold. We knew you were still alive, so we put you to bed. You've been in your cot resting ever since."

Jeremiah's eyes widened and he shook his head. "But I could have sworn I swam to shore? When did I surface?"

He looked down. "Never mind."

Miranda placed her hand on his shoulder. "You did go down, Jere. You were down there. You all were."

Jeremiah looked at Winston. "And you got the map?"

"To find the habitable zone, yes."

Jeremiah nodded slowly.

"The habitable zone. So that is what this trip is all about. This is why we came here." He pushed his way through Winston, Eli and Miranda and walked over to the other side of the tent. He was about to open the flaps when he turned around.

The three others were looking back at him, eyes wide open. No one was smiling. Just before Jeremiah left, he addressed them.

"Be ready to leave first thing in the morning."

The tent flaps closed and the three looked at each other and shook their heads.

Jeremiah walked over towards the campfire and found the bottle of whiskey still sitting in the sand.

There was about a third of the amber liquid left in the bottle.

He reached for it, pulled the cork out and tossed it out in the surf. He took a long swig, and winced as the potent alcohol burned his throat.

As the fuzziness took over, he flopped down in the sand. He set the bottle down and looked up at the sky. The star was there, and it looked more elongated; as if noble gases were reaching outwards from the core.

"Well, hello there, little star."

PART SIX

REVEALING
THE KEY

JEREMIAH FELL ASLEEP on the beach, and awoke the next morning to the others packing up the tent.

His head throbbed and his eyes felt puffy.

He staggered to his feet, and headed to the surf, and knelt down. He reached down and splashed some water in his eyes, wincing at the salt, but treasuring the refreshed feeling the seawater gave him.

"Miranda! Eli, Winston! Can you come here for a few minutes?"

He sat and looked out at the surf. The sky was lightening off in the horizon – just a pale blue – at the edge of sight.

He heard the others gather and sit down next to him. "Look out at the horizon," he said. "You see that? The light is coming. We don't have much time."

"To get back?" Miranda asked. "Shouldn't take us too long, I don't think. Not in the vehicles."

Jeremiah nodded. "True. Back to the colony, yes. But it's important we make it to the habitable zone before the sun brightens enough and the radiation levels rise again."

Winston stood and walked to the water's edge. "So we contact Abby before we leave. She can prep the colonists so they are ready to leave by the time we return."

Jeremiah nodded and accepted a bottle of water that Miranda handed him. "Thanks," he said. "You read my mind."

She smiled.

"Look up at the sky," Jeremiah said. "There it is. That's the neutron star."

Miranda gasped. "It's beautiful! It looks like a white blooming flower!"

"That's outbursts of gases," Winston said. "The star has collapsed and is dying."

Eli agreed the star looked beautiful. "But I remember science class," he said. "And a neutron star has a tremendous gravitational pull."

"Nelson said if we travel to the zone, we'll be protected from the star," Jeremiah said.

Winston scoffed. "How?"

Jeremiah shook his head. "He said we just have to have faith."

"Faith?" Winston sat and joined the others.

"We have to believe that he will be true to his word."

"So what do we do, Jeremiah?" Miranda asked.

Jeremiah stood up as the others looked up at him. "We contact Abby. She will need to organize the colonists and prepare the motor pool. We will meet her and continue to the zone."

"And what about the radiation?" Eli asked.

Jeremiah sighed and shook his head. "I don't know about that, Eli."

"Well how are we going to make the trip, then? Won't we have to wait for another six months? When it's dark again?"

Jeremiah looked directly at Eli. And then over at Miranda and Winston, who got to their feet as well. "Get up, Eli. We need to spring into action. He said we need to have faith. And that we will have all our questions answered when we get there."

Miranda looked back towards their gear and transport vehicles and then back at Jeremiah. "What about Cane?"

Jeremiah started to walk back to the camp. "We take him with us. He's in preservation wrap. No reason not to."

"What did he want, Jeremiah?" She started to follow him as the others joined. "What did he tell you?"

Jeremiah stopped walking, turned around and faced Miranda. "We take him with us."

As the sky slowly lightened, as the pastel blues started to appear over the days of their journey back to Miami, they paused each night and set up a far simpler camp.

As opposed to the network of tents they had set on the northern shore, they slept under the stars, as the temperatures were increasing dramatically and quickly as the light started to appear.

After the days' long journey, they finally saw the familiar skyscrapers, the former steel and glass cemetery rising from the brown, sandy dusty terrain.

In the distance, they saw transport vehicles, most of which looked like small tanks, with wheels like an automobile, lined up outside the outer gates of the compound.

They parked their vehicles next to the others. Jeremiah and Winston saw Counselor Abagail in the medical yard with hundreds of colonists waiting for medical clearance. The same tables were lined against the wall that Jeremiah remembered when he first arrived at the colony.

Doctors conducted impromptu exams as colonists formed lines.

Counselor Abagail spotted Jeremiah and Winston and headed over closer to them. "I got your message! All prepped and ready."

Jeremiah shook his head. "We don't have time for this, Abby!"

She shook her head and looked at Winston. "What are you talking about? This is standard procedure for everyone who leaves the colony."

"But this isn't a standard operation," Winston said. Jeremiah looked at him and nodded.

"We need to leave," Jeremiah said. "Nelson said we don't have much time."

"You said he left?" Winston asked.

"He said he was coming to join you," Counselor Abagail said.

"He never made it there," Winston said.

Jeremiah paused and looked at the hydraulic doors. Just inside was the medical exam area, and just beyond that, ME1.

Jeremiah walked into the medical receiving yard and stopped just a few feet from Counselor Abagail.

"You did a wonderful job, Counselor. And in such short time. But there is no need for the exams. How did you convince them all to leave the colony?"

"But will they survive the journey? Especially in the sunlight?"

Jeremiah looked at the transport vehicles lined up on the side of the compound. "We proceed. I know it's a leap of faith. But you have to trust me."

She pointed back at the colonists as her eyes widened. "And *they* have to trust me. They put their faith in me. They follow me just like that have you and Cane!"

Jeremiah sighed. He looked at the hydraulic doors again. Would this be the last time that they see the colony? Winston and Eli carried Cane on a long stretcher. "Where should we put him?" Winston asked.

"Just place him next to ROVER 1. And keep him out for a bit." Several of the colonists walked over, some looking down at Cane's wrapped body, others batted some tears.

"He really was loved and respected," Eli said. They carried his body across the medical yard to ROVER 1 as several of the colonists followed. Winston and Eli placed Cane's body on the ground in front of the massive vehicle, but kept it wrapped.

Jeremiah walked over and called Winston. He looked up at Jeremiah and raised his eyebrows.

"Do you think we should tell them?"

Winston nodded. "It's been a secret from them since we met in the conference room. Before the trip to the north. And, yes, I think they should know."

"But will they come? If they know the true fate of the planet?"

Winston shook his head. "I don't know, Jere. I honestly don't know. But like you told us. We have to trust you. You are our leader now. And you've been on your way to becoming our leader for the past several years. And if you say you can lead us to safety, then I am inclined to believe you."

Jeremiah called out to the colonists who had scattered about the medical yard.

"Our supplies have been loaded in the transport vehicles," he explained as people gathered closer around him.

One of the colonists stepped forward. He pointed up towards the sky as he spoke. "And so you say that this star – the one over there – is on a collision course with the planet?"

Jeremiah scanned the area. The colonists were many. Families who lived here together. Children who were born here. Elders who had died and were buried here. "I'm afraid it is so."

The same colonist pressed Jeremiah for more answers. "And so how is going to the habitable zone that you speak of a way to avoid the star?"

Jeremiah took a deep breath, and looked over towards Winston, Eli and Miranda, who stood off to the side.

Counselor Abagail was standing in the front row of the colonists. Jeremiah saw the concern in their faces. Ladies holding babies and biting their lower lip; men who rested their chins on their hands with eyes wide. People were fidgety, some looked up to the sky, and then back at Jeremiah.

Jeremiah exhaled and cleared his throat. "For some time now, you all have placed your faith in me as your leader. As you know, we unfortunately lost Cane on our mission to locate the map for the habitable zone. His body is on display near ROVER 1 for all who would like to pay their respects."

"And now, as your leader, I would like you all to listen to what I have to say."

Jeremiah watched as the colonists focused on him. He paused for a moment.

"When the scout first arrived at our colony, we did not know what to expect. He arrived seemingly near death, and we placed him in a coma. When he awakened, he had a private meeting with Desmond Cane, Counselor Abagail, Eli, Winston and myself. And in that meeting he told us about the star. This is something we knew about before the mission. And so the mission changed. We were challenged to find a map to the habitable zone."

"Now, what we discussed with you after the scout's arrival, was that the habitable zone is an area on the planet where there is still possibility of life. You all know the northern cities are flooded. We saw that first hand on our mission. We had to journey towards the bottom of the sea – where Philadelphia now lies – to locate the map we are now in possession of."

"But as I said, everyone, is that the objective of the mission changed –"

And then there was a mysterious male voice who interrupted Jeremiah: "– And that is because the habitable zone *does not exist.*"

Jeremiah turned to see the source of the mystery voice, as the crowd of colonists erupted in chatter.

He recognized the dark hair and warm, unshaven features.

Jeremiah's mouth dropped open. "Nelson?! You come here now?"

One of the colonists shouted. "You lied to us! The zone does not exist?!"

The scout raised his arms, as the colonists slowly quieted. He spoke loud, and with command. "No, the habitable zone does *not* exist. It was simply a rumor."

Jeremiah turned and listened to the scout as he started to speak.

"We are from the constellation Lyra and the star Vega. We've been watching you for several centuries now," Nelson said. "We're located about 25 light years from Earth, but we have the ability to travel beyond the physical, and we can telepathically transport our auras to this planet in little time. The neutron star which threatens your planet has been on approach for the better part of the time that we have been observing you."

"We are a rescue race. We populate our planet with refugees from not only the Milky Way galaxy, but Andromeda and other galaxies in interstellar space. We search for planets in distress."

The colonists remained speechless as Nelson continued.

"We have existed for millennia. I am fifth generation in my bloodline for rescue."

Nelson scanned the area and made eye contact with several colonists, and rested his eyes on Jeremiah. "Now let me be clear to all of you. This is a rescue mission. If you stay on this planet, you will be annihilated. That's why we built an arc ship for you. And we had to wait until your planet had reached a point where the majority of the population was already gone – and you are there now. You are surviving in small groups around the planet in pockets. For the amount of people that live on this ship is vast, but also finite."

Chatter erupted amongst the colonists as Counselor Abagail joined Winston, Eli and Jeremiah. Nelson walked over to the small group and leaned his head in their huddle.

"I had communicated with your previous leader, Desmond Cane, through a process we developed in your medical lab. We sent a scout back when your colony was first established, to develop a procedure to analyze one's mind. With that procedure, we can communicate with whomever we so choose."

Jeremiah paused for a moment and his face brightened. "I had that procedure. When I first arrived!"

Nelson looked at Jeremiah and nodded.

"Yes. I had discussed that with Cane on several different occasions. He chose you as his successor. That's why you had the procedure. We've been communicating with you ever since."

Jeremiah looked across the yard at Cane's body and swallowed hard. Nelson turned to the colonists and continued, speaking loudly as they quieted. "And so no, this habitable zone does not exist. There is no place on this planet that is left to go to. Your supplies have dwindled to almost nothing. Animal life is nearly extinct. Plant life is waning."

Winston raised a finger and Nelson nodded. "Why this moment? If you've know about this for hundreds of years, why come now? You chose this specific moment in time?"

Nelson nodded. "Yes. After your planet stopped its rotation, we proceeded with the construction of this ship. The arc I spoke of. We had to recreate the gravity that you are accustomed to on this planet. When you are inside the ship, the atmosphere will be completely identical to what you had been used to before your planet shifted. There will be houses, trees, roads and cars. Room for tens of thousands. That's why we waited. We had to time this with great exactness."

"Why is that?" Winston asked.

"If there were too many people still living on Earth, we would have to decide who is worth saving. And we are not qualified to make such a decision."

"Isn't every human life worth saving?"

He nodded. "Yes, but the problem that you have been dealing with is beyond our scope. We came because we are you. And you are us.

We have the technology to help. And our place is to save. But to make the choice – of who goes, and who stays on the planet and dies – is not a decision that can be made by you or us. And that is why we waited."

"And why the exactness?"

"We had to know we could land the arc when there was an estimated population of the planet that could fit on the arc. We didn't want you to have to decide who goes and who stays. That's why. There is a place prepared on the arc for each and every one of you. Just trust me. Have faith that you will be saved."

Jeremiah looked at Winston, and they made eye contact. "This is the faith versus science thing," Winston said.

Nelson turned his head around towards Jeremiah and Winston. "It's an interesting concept. And you can't have one without the other."

Nelson approached the exit to the medical yard as he let his message sink in. The colonists were surprisingly quiet.

"It's your choice, Jeremiah. I've given you the tools you need." And Nelson disappeared.

The last of the transport vehicles was loaded, as Jeremiah and Winston stood in the middle of the empty medical yard. They both looked around; the area, once teeming with activity, was now quiet, as the vehicles, lined up on the opposite side of the yard, were loaded with supplies, food, personal belongings, and 12 to 15 colonists in each.

"I think this is it, Jere. Sky is getting lighter."

Jeremiah turned around and saw the sky tinting a lighter blue on the horizon. "Still days away." He couldn't help but notice the star, which looked to him like a giant snowflake, as the gases continued spreading.

"And what about that star?" Winston asked. "How much time do you think we have with that?"

Jeremiah shook his head. "Still out by Jupiter. That could still be years away."

Winston nodded, patted Jeremiah on the back, as they headed over to ROVER 1. They climbed inside and shut the doors.

"Let's head out," Jeremiah said, as Eli turned around and nodded.

They had travelled for several days, and on even some points had not been able to get the map to function, but at the end of the fourth day, as the sky was starting to brighten more completely, at the crest of a barren, sandy hill, they got the first look at the ship.

And leading up to the ship were other motorcades. Thousands of vehicles, others arriving on foot. All heading to a giant, steel cylinder – which was so massive it reached nearly a mile towards the sky – and was so long the end was scarcely viewable.

Counselor Abagail gasped. "Look at all of them! So many colonies we didn't even know about!"

Eli nodded. "And he is rescuing all of them?"

Jeremiah leaned forward to see through the windshield. "Look at the size of that ship!"

The transport ship was larger than any ship they had ever seen before. It was nearly one hundred miles long, cylindrical, and mimicked the colonies they had constructed below ground on the planet: there was artificial light, parks and trees, even roads. The ship appeared large enough to have houses and apartments, and based on the sizes of the families and towns.

The motorcades filed in rows as there were different levitating signs for structured loading.

The sky danced with light.

It was not unexpected; and those who stopped running along the blue tinted fields craned their necks to see up to the sky: there was the star. They all knew it. And no one needed to speak.

For when the star became visible, when it entered the sky, the other millions and billions of tiny, white stars – the stars that were in systems so many light years away – the ones that seemed so out of reach – were now dwarfed by the star that now felt so close. The passage of night to day was becoming so grand.

Like it was there, reassuring, watching down on the people, looking at each of them, looking up at it, and letting them know that everything would be alright. And when the star brightened, fire shot out of the sphere, as if the flames were commanding the followers.

The fire reached across the night sky, soaring around the circumference of the planet, illuminating the sky as if it were daylight.

It appeared as if Earth had grown in size; the star was massive but did not hinder their view of the cosmos.

The other nearby planets – Mars and Venus in particular – became enlarged and gigantic in size; they filled the sky and those on the surface of Earth looked at each other with wide eyes, chatting and pointing towards the giant celestial planets.

"What is the star trying to show us?"

And then they waited at the entrance, looking back on the planet.

It really felt quite calm, quite serene.

As they looked out on the horizon, upon a view that they would never see again, as long as they lived, there was a certain aura of wonder that overtook the group. And wonder – so much wonder – of what was going to happen next.

They were ushered onto the ship, and when they crossed the threshold into the vast holding chamber, there were lengthy check-in desks.

ARRIVING

was illuminated on signs directing traffic among the thousands of arrivals.

Nelson approached Jeremiah and the others and smiled. "You see," he said. "This was so much bigger than just your colony. Now you see. Don't you?"

They looked up at the vast, cylindrical spacecraft, their mouths agape.

Jeremiah took Eli's hand as they looked up at the ship.

It was taller than any mountain they had experienced; it was a giant cylinder, which rotated slowly. They could not see the other end.

"And the ship rotates?"

There was a sense of uncertainty as the ship's thrusters ignited.

And when it lifted off of the Earth, they looked out through the observation deck, and saw the planet that had, recently, become so foreign and hostile to them. But now, as their feet left the soil, it hit home.

"Can we ever return?" Winston asked.

But there had been no answer.

They gestured towards the window, and then, as the ship cleared Earth's atmosphere, and started its journey away from Earth, there was an impenetrable silence that filled the observation deck, like a heavy blanket.

The blue marble, the providing planet that they all had known their entire lives, was now fading.

It was to be a trip across the cosmos; one of which none of them had ever taken before and would most likely never take again.

They could walk down streets of once familiar paved sidewalks (and play step-on-a-crack-break-your-mother's-back) but if one were to wander – and not very far – there would be expansive windows.

There would be giant views into the cosmos.

When they left the planet, it was not with the G-forces that man had been used to traveling into orbit with mankind on earth.

It was a graceful, gradual lift-off.

And when they had been, already, thousands of miles away, just minutes after leaving, and when Earth was the round, blue marble getting smaller and smaller, the population of the arc ignored the artificial trees; they did not care about the roads or the playgrounds.

Or the cars put into place to drive around the gigantic shuttle.

Or the houses, cafes, bars or libraries.

The survivors were not traveling the hallways. No one was in the mess halls or medical.

The thousands of survivors – all of those who had maintained in underground societies across a dying Earth, and who had made it to the ship, were perched at the windows, looking back at the blue sphere; one that was somewhat foreign from the land displacement, but, still, was the only thing familiar.

The expansive windows were miles long and high, with the survivors reaching out and everyone watching; everyone's face was pressed against the glass; their breath steaming it up in vapor.

But not a single person – not a single human being – ever lost sight of the celestial beauty; brightly blue, vastly changed, always beautiful.

THE END

The Vega Chronicles Will Continue

If you enjoyed The Wandering Star please leave a review on Amazon. And page forward to experience "The Tales of Tartarus" by Author A.L. Mengel.

Ashes

he night sky in Luxor revealed a vast array of tiny white stars, etched in the sprawling dark blue pallet. Antoine stood in a small clearing of sand in the middle of the desert, his arms crossed before his tall, dark stature - staring up at the stars, running through his mind, over and over, his plans for the future.

The cup was his.

Standing before the large sandy brown mountain, in front of the stone slab door covered in worn and painted hieroglyphics which informed the contents of the tomb:

Tutankhamen.

An enigmatic dark-skinned demon, Antoine stood over the excavation like a learned professor, wearing his signature long black coat. Suddenly, he broke his gaze to the stars. Shaking off his temporary distraction, he entered the dark abyss of the tomb.

329

"The Cup of Christ," he commanded to another immortal, who had been digging at the cave floor dirt with his hands. The follower looked up and snapped his head in the direction of Antoine's deep, booming voice of authority: "It's in the tomb with him. In the coffin."

Antoine pointed further into the compound, signaling with his hand that the place to dig was not out in the foyer but inside – in the inner chambers. The immortal immediately heeded the command and dropped the dirt he was holding, following Antoine like an obedient canine, crawling on the ground like an animal.

Antoine continued farther inside the tomb, through falling rock and sand, deeper until he was no longer able to walk. He was forced to drop to his knees and crawl. The floor of the cave was not soft and sandy. It was covered in rocks and small stones, and Antoine felt their small, determined solidity dig at his knees. But that did not deter his determined pace.

He climbed up a small mountain of rocks and boulders, discovering the first of the four rooms of Tutankhamen's final resting place. It seemed small and closet like with walls of clay and rock, and a small, square window towards the crest of the ceiling – signifying the possibility that this tomb once saw daylight before it was swallowed by the earth.

But what drew Antoine's attention was not the clay walls – it was not the oddity of the small window – not even the gleaming, dusty treasure which created a stark contrast to the dullness of the room – it was the four luminous gold coffins in the center of the treasure, standing guard as if they were elemental patriarchs.

Standing next to the coffin was another man holding a flaming torch, dressed similarly to Antoine, with the same long, dark and flowing hair and black coat – but this man had much lighter skin, perhaps like that of a European - with pronounced facial features and a slight lankiness about him. He was standing in the center of the room, staring up at the high ceiling, amidst a sea of golden treasure and coffins.

"Darius!" Antoine called shortly, descending a flight of stairs that was below the small opening towards the top of the room that he had to crawl through. "All I want is the Chalice. None of this is important."

"It's unbelievable," Darius said, shaking his head and staring at the coffin. The casket cast an aural yellowish glow in his face.

"What did you say?" Antoine called from atop the stone stairs.

Darius turned to face Antoine. "I was just saying it's amazing how the Cup of Christ got in there. Look at this!" Darius gestured his arm around the room. "All this treasure....it's so...old."

"Tutankhamen lived several thousand years before Christ," Antoine explained. "But time means nothing to her."

Darius lit another torch for Antoine. The treasures glistened in the light from the fire, sending a warm glow throughout the chamber. Darius turned to face Antoine, who had reached the floor, dusting the dirt of off his pants and jacket.

"Come now, Antoine," Darius said, helping Antoine clean himself up. "Do you think I have forgotten why we are here?" He turned to the nearest coffin, smirking as he did so. Darius walked to the center of the room, to the four gold painted coffins that were framed by the mountains of gold and jewels.

"There it is," he said, drawing his torch over the top, marking the correct coffin. "Tutankhamen. It is in there."

Antoine walked over to the coffin, quietly and reverently. "We need to open it. Night will be fading soon."

"Azra!" Antoine commanded, turning his head to summon the immortal. He came expeditiously, carrying with him a small brown leather bag, handing it to Antoine. Darius came over from his place at the coffin and took Antoine's torch.

Setting the bag on the floor, Antoine unzipped it and pulled out a long, dull tipped stake, and dug in the bag deeper for a small hammer.

Lining up the rounded point of the stake with the crease on the edge of the coffin – where the lid met the bowl – Antoine gave the hammer a loud bang! and a small shower of sparks poured down from the coffin.

The lid did not move.

Antoine continued and continued, causing some but not very noticeable damage to the artifact, sending loud booming echoes of the noise cascading to the top of the chamber.

After what seemed like several minutes of pounding and hammering, the top loosened somewhat; just enough for Antoine and Darius to bend over and take the lid with their hands try to lift it with all their immortal strength.

Thousands and thousands of years of dust billowed from the coffin like a giant cloud, and the lid that was sealed before Christ walked the earth was about to be opened.

The two immortals held the lid in their hands and stood above the coffin. As the air cleared they saw their prize: Tutankhamen. Holding the cup of Christ in his hand. When the lid was dropped to the floor with a crash and a large cloud of dust, Azra explained to them how the Cup of Christ managed to find its way into Tutankhamen's coffin. "Claret did it," he said.

"What I want to know," Antoine said, wiping the dust off of his hands, "is how Claret got that Cup in this coffin. I know she was infatuated with Christ, and I know that she killed Tutankhamen…but how did she do it? The two lived thousands of years apart. This Chalice would have been right here when Christ was supposed to have been drinking from it at the Last Supper. The Cup will tell me."

"Claret," Darius said, musing.

Antoine broke his gaze from the chalice and looked at Darius, expectantly.

"I haven't heard that name in quite some time," Darius admitted, speaking to Antoine. "She lived during the times of Jesus Christ. She had an obsession with Him. But how did it get here?"

Antoine reached in the coffin, carefully and respectfully amidst the remains of the boy-king, past the golden burial mask, and placed his fingers around the jeweled stem of the chalice. It stood out abruptly in this chamber of gold and jewels – it was a plain and simple chalice made of stone.

He held it up to the light of the torch. "This is the cup that will bring me eternal salvation," he said. "With this cup, we will no longer be damned. It is the key to our immortality."

Azra broke the silence that had permeated the chamber after Antoine had finished speaking. "They say that Claret still walks the Valley of the Kings. They say that she is still alive and walking the sands!"

Antoine eyes darted over to Azra for a moment, as if analyzing his comment. Saying nothing, he grabbed the brown bag from the floor and gingerly placed the chalice inside.

"This is all we came for," Antoine said. "We should leave now."

Azra was staring at the bag with wide eyes. Something was wrong. The cup lay in the bag as it should, but Azra did not take his eyes off it.

"You took his precious gift!" he screamed in horror.

Azra turned and ran, climbing up the stairs tripping over his legs, digging his way back through the opening to the cave, falling down the rocks below. Antoine and Darius stared at each other, without an answer for what just had happened.

As they lifted the coffin lid and placed it on the bowl, the ground began to shake. The massive earthquake shook the coffins off of the stone slabs that they had been resting on and the treasures surrounding the tomb fell and shook and dropped to the ground.

The ceiling showered dirt and rock on the two immortals, cascading a waterfall of earth and sand down below, quickly covering up the contents of the tomb.

"Quickly!" Antoine said. "Over to the stairs!"

Amidst giant boulders now falling from the top of tomb the two dashed to the foot of the stairs as the ground opened from beneath them, as the floor split in two – and flames shot out of the giant fissure. Climbing up to the entrance to the cave, Antoine turned and looked back at the room of Tutankhamen, staring at it one last time, in danger of being swallowed up into the bowels of the earth.

Fixated on the scene before him, he saw that the earth was furious, the room shook and the walls crumbled but the treasures and coffins did not die; they did not fall down into the fiery red abyss; they sat in place, as if standing command and protecting what was to be discovered.

But the angry flames died down just as quickly as they enraged. The giant cracks in the earth slowly began to fill in and close up and the coffins and treasure stood its ground.

The room was as they had come to it. There were no more flames. The coffins were placed on their stone slabs as they had found them.

Antoine snapped out of his stare at the whole scene. "What?" he asked himself, confused at the situation.

"What did you say?" Darius called back up from the bottom of the hill, continuing to the entrance to the cave.

"The tomb! It's like we never touched it!" Antoine slid down the hill, kicking up sand and rocks. When he got to the bottom, he stood up, dusted himself off, and joined Darius at the opening. The sky was still dark and filled with stars.

"When I looked back inside, the crack filled back in. The fire put itself out. It was like we were never there!"

The earth shook again.

This time much more intensely, shaking the two immortals off of their feet. The rocks around them began to loosen and sift, caving in and covering the entrance to the cave they had entered with giant boulders, rock and dirt.

And then the shaking stopped just as quickly as it had started. Lying on his back for a moment, he thought that maybe this was all a dream. He turned his head and looked over his shoulder, and saw what looked like no more than a mountain behind him. There was no cave opening; no hieroglyphics. It just looked like a brown, sandy stony mountain in the middle of the desert.

Darius shook his head, showering sand on the ground. Rising again to their feet, Antoine checked the bag he had carried from the tomb. There it was. The Cup of Christ, he thought. It wasn't a dream.

He really did have it. And Claret must be upset.

"We will see," Antoine said, as he and Darius walked from the cave, leaving what would become the archeological find of the century buried under rock and silt.

There it was behind them, as the two immortals glided away into the night, the entrance to Egyptian mystery and mythology swallowed by the earth, hidden from day and sun and light, preserving the mystery that wouldn't be discovered by mortals for over another century.

THE QUEST
FOR
IMMORTALITY

A Novel

A.L. MENGEL

THE SECOND BOOK OF THE
TALES OF TARTARUS

Stephen died on a Tuesday.

It was his destiny with death.

But still, he got his wish.

He didn't die in a hospital connected to machines.

He was in his backyard in the bright warmth of the sunlight, surrounded by his family and friends, and, just as he had requested, at the moment he passed and his death was declared, a flock of white doves was released, flying upwards towards the sky. Stephen's body lay on a large lounge chair, spread out and overlooking the expansive gardens that he had tended before his health had failed him.

Now that he was dead, the eyes that overlooked the yard saw nothing, but in essence, the presence of his body still took command of the gardens. And as the doves flew ever farther away, and spread out towards the blue heavens, there was a silence that fell over the small group on the terrace that sunny morning. As Stephen's closest family members fell into each other's arms in tears, not far from the lounge chair, Darius stopped and stared at his friend. He looked down at the frail arms, the sunken cheeks, and the sullen eyes.

He knew that Stephen had been ready for a long time.

For Stephen had been angry with the world since he contracted his disease, and ever since they had formed their friendship and fought together, he got another reason to live, to forage on, and to get just one more day in the world, even if the ending was inevitable.

~~*

The morning sun kissed the sky two days after Stephen died.

The warm rays touched the sidewalks and evaporated the morning dew, the orange fiery beams of light awakened the world, as the sky to the west gradually transformed from black, to blue, to pale to brilliant – and then to the growing shadows that ensued elongated; the warmth and the heat, the sweat and the caffeine.

The sun warmed the city during the midst of a wintertime cold front. It was a rare presence these days, and the citizens of Miami were out and about reveling in its warmth and hospitality, even treasuring the cooling shadows that each building formed as the sun rose farther into the sky. Some shoppers would find respite in the cool shadows, others sought the ocean and the beach. But there was one shadow that formed throughout the morning, somewhat separated from the others.

But it was there, and many didn't take notice of what created the shadow until they didn't want to face it.

It was the shadow of the Heavenly Slumber Funeral Home. It wasn't terribly large, considering it was a one-story building. But it was imposing nonetheless. And the shadow covered cars as they passed by. The shadow successfully blocked the sun, and, when one were to look at the front doors, one might wonder if there were a permanent shadow.

Stephen's body had arrived at Heavenly Slumber Funeral Home just before dawn from the Morgue. Ned McCracken was clutching the autopsy report in a manila folder in one hand, as he hovered over the body of Stephen Henry Drake. The report contained some hastily written notes, but what stood out to him was the cause of death, Pneumonia as a Complication of AIDS.

Ned McCracken grabbed a white coat, grabbed some rubber surgical gloves from the kit and placed them on each hand, paused and looked at Stephen's face.

The man looked at peace.

Very smooth skin on his face, thin lips, and manicured eyebrows. The eyes were already closed, but Ned secured them anyway with white medical tape, by placing a strip across each eyelid. He picked some cotton from a jar on the counter next to the preparation table, and pulled it apart into wispy strips. He stopped a moment at the lips.

The man seemed to be smiling.

Was he?

Ned looked throughout the preparation room.

The pale green tiles were the same that they always were. The room felt very clinical. Like it could have been in a hospital. There was the cold and dusty tile on the floor, the heavy, steel door with the small window in the center, and the stark, steel countertops.

The chill was always there.

The striking smell of alcohol, mixed with the stench of rotting flesh, and the overpowering scent of formaldehyde.

It was always there.

Everyday.

And when he left each night, he carried the smell with him on his clothes.

The smell of death.

He couldn't get away from it. It followed him everywhere. But he knew this was the life that was he was meant to live.

And then Ned looked down at the body again. At Stephen.

What did you do, my friend? To get something as devastating as AIDS?

But the man seemed to be at peace.

He longed not to disturb that peace, but he needed to fill the cheeks. They were sunken dramatically on both sides, to the point where the cheekbone was highly visible through the thin layer of flesh. This man was clearly dying for a long time.

Ned shook his head and paused for a moment. He took a deep breath and exhaled. Some of these cases were some of the most complex. AIDS, Cancer. They were all wasted away. And it was his job to make them look like they did before they got sick. So he fished for some gloves from the box on the counter, and started to pry open the lips.

Dead skin.

The cold, hard, uninviting flesh of the corpse. Tough, firm, cold.

It was so difficult to manipulate, to form into something that wasn't horrific.

He knew that he had to handle the face with care. For if he didn't finish this task soon, the face would freeze in a state of surprise and that just wouldn't do. The time to manipulate the skin and flesh and prep the body for viewing was very finite. And Ned knew that he couldn't waste any time with this one. The corpse came in wasted away, and he had to fill the fill and get it ready for display.

That was the everyday task at Ned McCracken's job.

As he stood over the body, bending down towards the face, he took great care in parting the lips, and the jaw, using both hands to pry each layer of lips and teeth away from each other, he placed a wad of cotton in the left, and then the right cheeks. He removed his hands and let the jaw close.

He stood back for a moment and looked down at Stephen.

Ned nodded for a moment, and reached down to adjust the chin. He stood back again and studied the corpse. His forehead wrinkled and he reached up and stroked his chin. "More to the right," he said, and reached down again, pried open the jaw, and stuffed some more cotton on the right side of the mouth.

"There."

He stood back to admire his work.

THE BLOOD DECANTER

A Novel by

A.L. MENGEL

Miami.

The Devil's city.

The land where the sun sets later, and the days are hotter, brighter, sweatier, and filled with more caffeine. Where the tall royal palms line the sidewalks; where the manicured lawns are a deep, forested green all twelve months of the year; where the water remains blue and bright and brilliant.

But the darkness of the Devil –

Miami.

It's the crystalline jewel on the tip of the Atlantic coast – hugging the Caribbean, surrounded by tropical waters and majestic million dollar mansions that line the docks and the inter-coastal waters which were usually scarcely used, except by Hollywood elite and celebrities. Most of the time, the waterfront palaces remained empty. And not far from the mansions and high-rises one finds the tiny, shoebox single level cement homes, dirty, bars covering the windows, litter on the lawns and too many cars parked along the streets.

Ah, Miami.

The brightest city with the darkest shadows. Yes, the city has a dark side. But it's the place that I call home. The place where I work; where I follow my calling. The city I love, and have come to love. And it's the city where I truly feel that I came face to face with the Devil himself...

Read these novels and other exciting stories from Parchman's Press

www.ingramcontent.com/pod-product-compliance
Lightning Source LLC
Chambersburg PA
CBHW050917250626
47155CB00001B/275